2023 SCI-FI ANTHOLOGY

SHORT STORIES BY SELECTED AUTHORS

E. J. RUNYON

S. A. GIBSON

PUBLISHED BY SCIENCE FICTION NOVELISTS 2023

CONTENTS

Introduction   v
The Editors   vii

HUNGER   1
Marc Neuffer

THE COMITTEE   7
D. J. Camden

TIME SEEDS   19
Marc Neuffer

THE GHOST AND THE MACHINE   25
Christina Engela

ANGELIC   36
David Booker

I, MAC   41
Christina Engela

DINNER WITH THE DOGE   58
Howard Loring

CONTACT   77
Phillip Cahill

HERBERT   90
D. J. Camden

A GAGGLE OF GHOSTS   97
David Booker

RESOURCE MANAGEMENT   105
Philip Cahill

NEVER ACCORDING TO PLAN   114
M. J. Konkel

THE BOTTOM LINE   124
Eric Richard Gabrielsen

STEEL AGAINST STEEL   134
S. A. Gibson and R. J. Davies

HOW IT ALL STARTED   152
Howard Loring

COCOON   168
Scott Cirakovic

UNDER A CRETACEOUS SUN   178
M. J. Konkel

Thank You   207

INTRODUCTION

For the Science Fiction Novelists Facebook group, we love posting our annual calls for submission. This year's crop surprised us in its wide and varying tales. From harder Sci Fi, to time travel, alt future worlds, and clone worlds, to farce, we offer our finest from 2023. Our group offers you imagination and excitement—though some of us may have destroyed few universes along the way.

Each year, we challenge our members to submit their newest short stories. Gathered here are the imaginary worlds we create and have access to via our online world: Seventeen stories from eleven authors, with reach beyond your standard hard science fiction. Each story takes you by the hand into unique worlds.

Significant credit goes to our two professional editors, EJ Runyon (Development) and Susan Soares, also members of the group who provide their services at special rates. Bringing you this, our third volume, we hope our authors bring you stories you'll remember and reread again and again.

Come and explore these newer 2023 worlds.

A NOTE ON LANGUAGE

The Science Fiction Novelists group has members based all over the world who write in a variety of English dialects. This anthology features stories (and spelling) in British English and American English.

THE EDITORS

EDITOR IN CHIEF: S. A. GIBSON

S. A. Gibson has published more than ten books and several short stories, many co-written. Most stories are set in a future which has lost its advanced technology because of a catastrophic viral pandemic that has led to the collapse of modern civilization. Gibson uses his PhD in education to blend technological and historical research with creative ideas. Find out more about his work at www.protectedbooks.org.

DEVELOPMENTAL EDITOR: E. J. RUNYON

E. J.'s writing guides are *Tell Me (How to Write) a Story*, from Inspired Quill out of the UK, and *5 Ways of Thinking to Change Your Writing World Around* from Protected Books, in California.

She also has four well-regarded novels out from small indie presses. She's run the Bridge to Story website since 2010, where she coaches live, via Skype, and story edits both novices and published authors. Her life's goal is sharpening your stories into something deeper, to give your readers satisfying storytelling. Being notoriously *lysdexic*, E. J. never offers to proofread or line edit.

You can find her on social media, or at her website, which offers 52 free writing lessons: www.bridgetostory.com.

HUNGER
MARC NEUFFER

Author of eight novels, Marc Neuffer uses his extensive science and engineering background to pen novels of future time and space with plausible science as a backdrop for his imaginative character-driven stories. Before becoming an author, Marc spent twenty years roaming the world with the US Navy as a nuclear propulsion engineer. He has lived in San Diego, Los Angeles, San Francisco, and Seattle. After retiring a second time, he bought a piano and started writing fun-read science fiction novels. In retirement, with nothing else left on his bucket list, he dreams of future things to come.

All my nights are dark and stormy. Dark by distance or by rotational effect, turning from the light. Stormy from roiling internal demons come to haunt me after the visual distractions of the day have faded. It's when I do my best work.

"Captain, you have a message waiting."

"Who's it from?"

"Captain Fwala, the male you had…"

"Yeah, yeah. Erase that from your memory."

"Erased."

"All right, pipe it to me." I counted to three before a vaporous hologram head emerged in my sightline. This ship's new AI is too formal for my taste. It insists on calling me Captain even though I'm the only one aboard. I need to dig into its settings when I have more time.

"Sahza!" it said. "So good to see you, if only as a ghost. I fondly recall our last port call together—"

"Get to the point, Fwala. I'm on a schedule here." I'm not, but there's no need for Fwala to know my business.

"I'm calling in that little favor you owe me."

I let a fake thoughtful pause pass before I respond. "Okay, what do you want?"

"I find myself in a teeny, tiny bit of a quandary."

His topknot twitches, a sure tell he's lying. "Go on."

"I need to make a vector change to Vanklu, just business, of course. I have a passenger aboard who wouldn't be well received there. You know how hyper-xenophobic they are. My passenger must go to a light grav colonized world for oxygen breathers. A G12 planet. I'm hoping you can take it somewhere suitable. I'd be remiss in my duties if one of my passengers was… Well, you know the Vanklu."

"I don't know why you trade with them." Something smells rotten here. "Are you carrying some proscribed elements for them? You know the guild will bust your ass big time for that, Fwala. Does this… thing need any special environment? Will it stink up my ship? What does it eat?"

"It can easily tolerate your ship's environment and eat what your processors can produce. I'm sending you a video, along with its dietary preferences."

The lifeform seems bilaterally symmetrical on its exterior with sensory organs at the top end as far as I could determine. "What's that thing called? I've never seen one before. It looks harmless enough."

"It calls itself a Canadian, but it's a human, a young female

2

of its race. They've recently arrived in this sector—still have that new species smell."

"Never heard of them. Okay, I'll bring it aboard, but after this, we're square. Clean start. Back to zero energy ground state."

"Thank you. May you forever change for the good."

"Yeah, yeah. I said yes. Enough platitudes. How soon do you want to dock up? I need time to shift into a form that pasty thing can identify with. Is it always that hairless?"

"I can make rendezvous with you in three days. That should be plenty of time. I'm sending over the translator files, so you'll be able to understand it. Be prepared for a chatty visitor."

Before I can respond, Fwala signs off. I hate shifting on short notice. Given more time, it would be a less painful transition. My natural form usually scares the crap out of most two-eyed bipedal types or at least makes them uneasy, looking over their shoulders as they hide the young.

* * *

When the inner airlock door slides open, there it stands, boxy luggage in each hand—a fragile pink thing, yellow hair pulled tightly back from its face, its mouth such a bright red, I mistake it for blood. I wonder if Fwala has been skimping on its rations. "Welcome aboard... ah... I didn't get your name. Do you have one?"

"It's Amy and thank you SO much! I didn't know what to do when the captain told me about, you know, about those icky... the Vankle. I remember once when my friend Wendy and I got separated and—"

"Okay, okay. You can finish your story later after you're out of the airlock. Step aside. I need to close this hatch. It's the Vanklu, by the way." I wonder if the ship gravity is too low for this hopper. "Your quarters are the first hatch on the left...

That way. No, the other left." She bounces with every step, and that swaying length of gathered hair on the back of her head is annoying to watch as she saunters away. I think I'll cut it off.

Passing her hatch, I take a quick look. She stands in the middle of her bunk space, one hand on her hip, the other pressed against a corner of her thin mouth as if making decorating choices. I hit the close actuator. Let her figure out how to open the damn thing. I have work to do.

* * *

"So, you see, I'm traveling to join my daddy. He's working for our ambassador on, oh, I get the names all wrong sometimes. I think it's the planet Barrel or Bartle or Bramble... something like that. Anyway, I had to travel at a moment's notice, leaving behind most of my wardrobe. The local authorities insisted I be on my way. I have the cutest long frock. Jenny says she doesn't think it is, but I think she's just jealous of me being friends with Suzy. You'd like Suzy. She lives on Veeder or Ventor now and has SO many boyfriends. I don't know how she keeps them straight. It's probably because her family's so rich, but Becky says—"

"STOP. Don't you need to breathe occasionally?"

"Yes, I breathe all the time. Momma says proper breathing is a sign of good breeding, that and posture, and of course, the cultured walk..." Her voice trails off as I make my way out of the galley. Three months of this could very well drive me insane.

* * *

I've found a solution—other than placing her in stasis or strapping her to the ship's hull. The thing has quite an interest in visual entertainment media, staying silent, mesmerized in front of the screen for hours. I need to look up more about her species. If they're all like this, it won't be long before someone comes along and cancels their ticket. Speaking of which, hers will bring me a nice bonus at the other end.

* * *

Well. That lasts about two weeks. Now she wants to know everything. Not just about me, my ship, my species... everything. It's no use directing her to the data banks. She can't read gen-text, and I'm not about to show her how to activate the audio on that thing.

I've banned her from the bridge. Regulations, I told her. It's the only place I can sleep in peace now. She holds continuous conversations with herself, or perhaps she thinks I'm paying attention. I'm going to slip some sleepy-time in her tea.

* * *

We've been diverted. Her father has moved on to another planet. In his place, I would too, just to stay ahead of Amy and her chattering. Another month now added... Not a good thing. I need to molt soon, and I can't do that in my present form.

Amy's talking points have no start, no endpoints, and if there's a discernable middle, I can't find one. She goes on and on about how strange every other race is, throwing out pejorative evaluations in solar bursts. She's not too enamored by many of her own kind either, especially those she calls The French. I'm considering taking out a contract on her momma if she mentions her one more time.

* * *

It just proves, like an ever-present stench, your senses eventually become dulled to the stimulus of irritating beings. I'm beginning to have a less intense dislike for this thing, though ugly as she is. In self-defense, I've boosted the carbohydrate levels in her food. It seems to calm her.

It's a race against time, and time has won. I have to molt. There's no choice. If we hadn't been diverted, I would have been rid of her well before my change comes. I have become a bit fond of Amy and the background noises she produces during our time together. It's that insatiable hunger after molting, you know. She would have lived longer if I hadn't been so hungry. The kind of hunger that makes you want to burn planets. It's a craving, like a desperate need for liquid ammonia.

Since I haven't registered her as a passenger in the transit data banks, she still appears on Fwala's manifest. He's going to be pissed when he finds out. I'll owe him another favor. So much for our clean start. Anyway, I need to get back on track with my current contract. There's a small moon that needs destroying, and I'm in such a foul mood, I may not give those squatters a second warning to vacate. I've tacked her ponytail to the corner of my rear viewscreen as remembrance of the soft, chatty thing called Amy.

THE COMITTEE
D. J. CAMDEN

DJ Camden lives in Auckland, New Zealand. He works outdoors doing environmental restoration, which has provided a certain scepticism of humanity's place on this planet. But also hopes for the future. He has written two self-published novels, but short stories are a lot of fun.

"Thank you for manifesting here and now," said the giant Banyan tree at the summit of Olympus Mons. "Your presence is an indication of the importance of simulation 96. Otherwise known as Earth."

The Banyan's roots splayed out across the dusty red rocks like giant fingers. Its limbs waved delicately as it admired the view. Occasionally, a dry leaf would detach and drift gently away across the red plains of Mars. Above and around the tree constellations shimmered billions of sharp twinkling points. The Milky Way stretched across the space above, and the subject solar system was all around them. Eight planets and their many chaperones circled the Sun. Earth glowed bright blue and white as it rolled through its prescribed orbit.

Gathered around the Banyan tree were the rest of the committee. A π symbol, a recurring explosion, an angular model spacecraft, and a beautiful, androgynous humanoid. Hanging from the branches of the Banyan were two more committee members, a sloth, who appeared to be sleeping, and a monkey.

"This meeting is presumptuous and pointless," said the explosion, a constantly erupting mushroom cloud made up of rolling fire and spitting debris. "The only reliable constant in the universe is chaos. This should be the same for any simulation. Making decisions on rules and procedures governing this sim is misleading and insulting and a waste of my time. Sim96 is not important. We are not important. I only came here to remind you all of this."

"This simulation is pure. Maybe the only purity in our universe," said the humanoid. "Our sims have rules, parameters, objectives, beginnings and endings. And this sim does our work for us. Philosophically, technologically, and evolutionary. Sim96 is exceptional. It has already provided framework for our own lives. It's the opposite of the chaotic nihilism you seem to purport." The humanoid walked slowly around the explosion, batting away small flecks of fiery debris with casual disdain. "And you're wrong. The only constant in this universe is mathematics."

The explosion appeared to inhale, sucking in clouds of fuming gas and red dust. "Almost all our sims eventually descend into chaos. This is the primary lesson we have learnt from these experiments, that only a tiny percentage evolve to survive in their simulated universe. All the rest of them manage to destroy themselves with a variety of innovative methods. This is what they're good at, and this one is no different. It's not exceptional. It's certainly not pure. You're too involved. Look at you, you might as well be one of them."

"You may call me Eden," said the humanoid with a sardonic smile. "Please refer to me as such."

"Eden, you pompous idiot, you are too entangled with your own creations. You have lost perspective. You're losing touch with the base reality. Look at what happened to Monkey." The explosion exhaled and expelled fiery balls of debris into the space above, some falling on the Banyan tree. Monkey looked up, a confused look on his simian face, before going back to foraging for fleas in his hairy crotch. The sloth stayed blissfully asleep.

"Base reality?" scoffed the spacecraft. "Surely our simulations have proven that none of us can be sure of base reality. We're all living in a game. We might as well play the game. Manipulate it. Enjoy it. See where it takes us." The spacecraft gained speed as it circled the group. Complicated projectile weapons of various sizes clicked into place around its hull. "Are we any different from Sim96? How can we be sure we're not little codes of data also? Base reality is long forgotten. No one can prove it even exists."

"I can be sure," said π. "I am the designer. I built this sim. I maintain the memory, the hardware, and the substrate required to run it and many others. I'm the only one of us that has proof that it's real." The π symbol expanded and contracted as it spoke, "And, this sim is already at capacity. Ten billion humans is the limit."

"I don't believe your machinery exists; it's probably just a construct of your narrow-minded intellect." The spacecraft cut lines through the space around the group, occasionally firing a volley of missiles over the highest reaches of the Banyan tree. "Of course, we're living in a simulation, just like those pathetic little humans. It's just a lot bigger. Whoever is running our sim must have infinite resources. The rules of our universe are proof it's a simulation. The limits of light speed, thermodynamics, gravity, and the dark matter holding it all together. Numbers rule our universe, and these numbers are proof that it's a sim. Once you accept that, you realise that nothing matters. We might as well do whatever the hell we want. Have as much fun as possible because nothing is real. Maybe life begins in the moment we realise we don't have one."

"I disagree," the explosion countered. "Creation is nothing but chaotic coincidence. Look at where we have manifested. This mega volcano haemorrhaged lava for hundreds of millions of years and made Mars tilt on its axis. This reality can't possibly be a sim. There's too much chaos."

"The dullest minds are always sceptical of simulation theory. Because it makes a mockery of their lifelong pursuit of knowledge and understanding. Here and on Earth," said the spacecraft, somehow managing to exude caustic sarcasm while flying around the group.

"We're not here to debate the nature of our own existence," said the Banyan. "There's another committee for that. We need to decide what to do with Sim96. The humans are beginning to question their belief in the stability of their own reality. Our subjects are in the process of creating their own simulations. Their devices are already extensions of their minds. Each individual human is already running their own simulations in their heads. The way their brains interpret what they see. This is a sign that Earth is close to reaching its logical conclusion. As π said, humans will have to stop their population expansion to maintain the integrity of the sim, or a reset will be required."

"Let it run," said the explosion. "Let us see where these chaotic little creatures end up. They may even survive."

"Yeah, let it run," the spacecraft agreed. "They will probably destroy themselves. If we really need to reset, I can always intervene and manipulate them into a near extinction event. It'll be fun."

The Banyan ignored them. "π, what will happen if the human population continues to grow?"

"The sim will fail, and the humans will see the cracks in their reality. It's already beginning to happen. When they meditate or take the right psychoactive drugs that unlock certain parts of their brain, they can see the fabric of the universe. A fleeting glimpse of the machinery, the pixels and geometric patterns that make up the planetary simulation we call Earth. What they call déjà vu is a glitch in the code causing repeats. When the code fails, the existing humans will become stuck in a repeated pattern. Endlessly re-living the same moment over and over. The glitch will become their reality, and all my work will be meaningless," said π.

There was silence as the Banyan surveyed the committee. They didn't appear to be listening to π who flickered through shades of red, indicating its annoyance.

"They have exceeded their parameters," π continued, raising its voice. "The time has come to disassemble them. Send them all back into the quantum foam. Feed their atoms back into the engine of cosmic inflation and build a *new* sim. An improved sim. Under my supervision."

"This is what we must decide. Reduction, intervention, or annihilation. Is there more to be learned from Sim96? Is it worth continuing?" asked the Banyan. "Remember why we activated this sim in the first place."

There came a long silence. The Banyan regarded Earth, glowing with health in the distance. Around them the universe was bright and active. Nebulas pulsed with contracting stardust. Distant galaxies wheeled around their central black holes. Globular clusters radiated concentrated light, and supernovas sparkled with harsh incandescence. Around them, the surface of Mars glowed red as it descended into darkness. Olympus Mons was so big, it eclipsed the horizon. Eden shrugged and shook their head.

The silence continued as the sloth seemed to lose its grip, almost falling out of the tree, one clawed limb barely hanging on. "Entertainments! Thass whass this sim is for. Spure entertainmentss." The sloth slurred as it swung itself back up onto the Banyan to promptly fall asleep again.

"No," said the Banyan. "It's not for entertainment. Sim96

has already provided important data on carbon-based evolution, bio-intelligence, artificial intelligence, and various theories on our own long-forgotten past. Question is, can it still provide reliable data? Or has it reached its use-by date."

"I agree with Sloth," said the spacecraft. "All your derived data, all your pattern recognition and repetition, all your theories on evolution are meaningless and boring. We might as well do what we want with these little humans. Have some fun with them."

The Banyan shook its limbs in agitation. Monkey hooted with laughter, and the sloth raised a sleepy eyelid. "We all know you've already been having fun with them. We recognise your clumsy attempts to intervene, from Genghis Khan to Hitler. Never mind your latest experiment with this Trump character."

"Isn't he great? I have high hopes for him. And he's only just getting started." The spacecraft spun and launched another volley of missiles over the Banyan treetops.

"It's a laboratory. It should be orderly and methodical," said π. "Your interventions have contaminated the petri dish and made our findings unreliable. If you want entertainment, go and create your own sim."

"Thass entertainmentss," slurred the sloth as it lost its grip and fell from the Banyan tree, disappearing before it hit the ground. The group fell silent again.

"Sloth's probably gone back to his eternal pleasure space," said the spacecraft. "Seems like a good idea."

"Please, let's try to maintain focus. We have a decision to make," said the Banyan. "Do we try to contain them, somehow stop and reverse their population growth to maintain operational integrity? Or reset, recalibrate, start again with some primitives? Or do we shut it all down and officially end Earth? As I mentioned earlier, they're almost at the point of creating their own simulations. Once that happens, we must turn them off."

"Why should that be the termination point?" asked Eden. "Why can't they be allowed to achieve their own god-like powers? In the end, if you can believe any satisfactory explanation of existence, simulated or not, it's sacred. It teaches empathy. These humans are not less real but more real, animated by their environment but also universal forces. Leading to the belief in a creator. A belief in us. Religion with a new technological name."

"He who believes in Me will live a good life!" shouted Monkey.

"Oh God, you've done it now," muttered the explosion.

"He who eats My flesh and drinks My blood has eternal life, and I will raise him up on the last day. I am the bread of life. He who comes to Me will not hunger, and he who believes in Me will never thirst!" Monkey pointed a crooked finger as he spoke. His furrowed brow framed a confused expression.

"He lost his mind after that Jesus character died. I don't know why you invited him," said the explosion.

"He was part of the original committee, when we created Earth, and we need to keep him involved, if only to keep an eye on him," said the Banyan.

Monkey investigated his navel with forensic attention. Concentrating, with his hooked finger, pulling out a large flea, examining it as he held it between his nails. Then eating it gleefully. He looked around as he chewed. "For God so loved the world that he gave his one and only Son, that whoever believes in him shall not perish but have eternal life!"

"He was the one that put that Jesus character on Earth, to get them all to worship him. Then he became seduced by the sim, falling into it even deeper than Eden. He believes he is their God. He believes the ridiculous stories they wrote about him. His insanity is of his own making," said the explosion.

"The one true God is the sovereign Creator! He is spirit! He is eternal! The one true God possesses all knowledge and all power, is present in all places. There are many false gods, but none of them possess the attributes of the one true God!"

Eden sighed and shook their head sadly. "He used to be so creative and powerful. I wonder if I can help repair his mind." They walked under the Banyan and tried to coax God down.

The spacecraft hovered in front of the tree. "It was when millions of humans started praying to him. He thought they were talking to him, he thought they needed him. He took it personally, but he couldn't cope with their adulation, or their demands. He was once their God. Now he's a Mad God." The spacecraft reconfigured its weaponry. "It's good that he's here. It's a reminder to all of us to keep perspective. Not to get too emotionally involved. This is, after all, just a game."

"We are Gods to these humans." said Eden, "We have a certain responsibility. I want to see them prosper. I want to see them evolve. I want them left to their own devices. We should increase the scope of the sim to allow this."

"You are worse than God," said the explosion. "You have been seduced by their erroneous veneration as well. Those stupid humans invent creationism to explain what they can't understand, and you assume they have recognised you. Look at you, taking on their form. Your arrogant assumptions undermine the whole experiment. Because remember this is just an experiment."

"I'm just asking why can't we let it continue? Why should we be restricted by physical limitations? There is more to learn from these humans." Eden swept their manicured fingers through their platinum-blond hair and smiled enigmatically. "And I like this form. Its symmetry is beautiful."

π changed colour to a pulsing orange. "You all don't seem to realise what it takes to run this sim. Remember, every human, every animal, every rock and tree and chunk of dirt is a single piece of code running in my processors. This is a physical requirement which you seem to have forgotten. The energy demands are huge, the logistics of maintaining the hardware requires constant attention. It's already the size of a small moon, draws enough energy to deplete a sun, and it's becoming impossible to dissipate all the heat exhaust. It's at breaking point. If Sim96 continues to expand, if the humans continue to procreate, then the machinery will fail."

The rest of the committee didn't appear to be listening. The spacecraft amused itself by firing missiles over the nearby caldera. The explosion had grown to a towering dark mushroom cloud. Eden was staring intently at their pocket mirror and applying makeup while God continued to search for fleas. There was no sign of the sloth's return.

"To continue Sim96 at the current rate of expansion, we would need to convert another moon or large asteroid into processing substrate. Expansion would take time. The logistics are challenging."

The silence continued. The spacecraft aimed its weapons high above the system of caldera's where the committee had gathered and unleashed another barrage of missiles. The weaponry exploded above them and showered them all with bright colourful flares like fireworks. Sparks drifted down amongst them like burning rain. The Banyan tree rustled its leaves in annoyance. "When a sim is on the verge of creating its own simulations, that's where it must end. We can't have sims stacking within sims. They will just end up repeating themselves and wasting our resources. This is the hard problem of consciousness."

"Humans have been wondering if their world was real for as long as their existence, as long as they have been dreaming. The simulation theory is still the oldest explanation in the book. They were always going to evolve to the stage where they create their own virtual worlds. Aspiring to become the gods they so admire," said the spacecraft. "This inevitability was easy to predict even without a sim. And being so crushingly boring, that's why I intervened and introduced some individuals to change the course of their history. To shake things up a bit. Make the game a bit more entertaining."

"You jeopardized the integrity of the sim and made the results unreliable. Your behaviour was irresponsible in the extreme," said π. "Not that anyone seems to care."

"We still haven't reached a decision," the Banyan sighed. "As chairman of the committee, I have a responsibility to our superiors to facilitate a satisfactory outcome. I propose we turn it off. We have derived as much useful data from Sim96 as is possible. Earth has outlived its usefulness, and it's time to move onto another project."

The silence weighed heavy as the committee members amused themselves. Eden had coaxed God out of the tree and was brushing his hairy back. The explosion had reduced itself to a small, red smoulder while the spacecraft floated stationary facing the Banyan.

Eventually, π agreed, "Sim96 has exceeded its parameters to the point where its subjects have become agents of chaos. The data is unreliable. Also, certain members of this committee don't seem to understand the purpose of this sim. They don't respect the boundaries and don't appreciate the work I do maintaining it. I vote for dissolution."

As π spoke, the explosion burst into life again. A booming noise echoed around them as the explosion erupted into the space above. The fiery ball glowed like a small sun, stationary as it reached the apex of its trajectory. Then it fell upon the Banyan tree, setting the entire tree on fire.

"Very amusing," shouted the burning tree above the crackling flames. "Is that your answer?"

"I don't care about your rules and regulations. I don't care about Sim96 either. But I would rather see it descend into chaos than conform to your sterile bureaucracy," said the explosion.

At the same time, the spacecraft unleashed a volley of

missiles at π. The symbol remained intact but was engulfed in flames and smoke.

"I will not stand for such disrespect!" fumed π, now on fire. "You are on your own. See how you fare without my help, you ingrates!" π disappeared from the space, leaving a puff of smoke.

"Now see what you've done," said the flaming Banyan. "We needed someone to run the hardware, π was the only one willing to do the mundane tasks of maintaining the machinery. Without its supervision, Sim96 will descend into chaos and eternal glitches. And π was the only one capable of actually turning the thing off!"

"We came from chaos, and everything eventually returns to chaos," said the explosion, still burning its way through the limbs of the Banyan. "Life and death is chaotic. From the birth of an insect to the birth of a star. This is the way the universe works." The explosion slowly reversed. Extinguishing itself and inhaling into a smaller surge, until it was a tiny flame that shimmered on a charred Banyan twig, then flickered out of existence.

"What am I supposed to tell our superiors?" Shrugged the smouldering Banyan, shaking the last of its flaming leaves from its frame. "We were supposed to come to an agreement and act on it. I need your decisions. I need this signed off. This makes me look incompetent."

"I really couldn't give a shit," said the spacecraft. "You probably *are* incompetent. I'm off to find another sim to play with." Flaring its engines and scribing a circle around the Banyan, it powered off towards the nearby Andromeda constellation.

The Banyan's burning limbs drooped with exasperation. Eden glanced at the tree while whispering conspiratorially into God's ear. They took God by the hand and slowly walked away.

"Are you two abandoning me also? Does no one have any respect for democracy and process anymore?"

Eden looked over their shoulder and smiled. Their eyes glowed red, and their platinum-blond hair had curled up into two spiky little horns. "Don't worry about Earth. God and I will guide them through the times of tribulation ahead. We're the only ones who truly care about this sim, and we have their best interests at heart. They will be rewarded for their faith in us."

The Banyan stood alone at the summit. Its leaves had been burned away, and its limbs, still charred, kept smouldering. It despondently watched them leave. Eden and God appeared to be laughing together as they walked slowly down the slope of Olympus Mons.

TIME SEEDS

MARC NEUFFER

I've stood at the rail every evening since we arrived. If it weren't for the burrowing vermin, the sunsets would be a magnificent transition into night viewed from land—night is when they come out and the reason we stay on the ship after sundown. We've seen a few Gooser vermin during the day, but those are sluggish, torpid, easy to kill—a pike thrust into their brains. At night, we're safe aboard our vessel, stone-anchored in the bay, sails reefed. They don't swim.

I've come to like this pleasant place of cooling trade winds, predictable rains, and lush vegetation in the last four months. This is a suitable planet, except for the nagging wonder of where all the higher-level intelligent natives go.

"Have you come to a preliminary recommendation yet?" Ernie asks from his usual spot next to me, looking toward the land.

"No, not yet, but soon after we get back, after the data review."

Two weeks remain, and we still don't know who built what are now ruins or the stone piers, though it was undoubtedly a long time ago. The Goosers hadn't made them—those meter-long terrors don't use tools beyond their digger claws that can rip the flesh from your bones in less than a second if you get too close. Bethany named them on the first shore day when she was startled by a pair emerging from their day hole.

This wooden deck is my preferred place to muse, to objectively mull over the day's findings. Chafed and worn from the ropes and chains we haul up to bring the mud-core samples aboard, my hands rest on the thick deck railing. It's this place amidships where I enjoy the slow, undulating roll of the ocean swells, tamed by the remaining barriers once constructed to form a seaport.

Ernie speaks the question that's been on all our minds. "Could this place have been seeded before we arrived?"

"Possibly. But we haven't found any evidence of that. Even if it had been, it didn't stick. I think we have an excellent project candidate."

"Well, it'll be good to get back. These natural-fiber clothes give me the worst itch."

Knowing it's temporary, no one on our team objects to them. Some enjoy roughing it. We accept the imposed restrictions. No technology beyond what the probes assessed as probable native materials is permitted; in our case, a wooden ship, iron nails, and not-so-iron men and women. The initial orbital probes find piers, quay walls, and a few unnatural piles of squared-up rock—deserted. Even the remaining towers barely resemble built things. Our landing team finds no monuments or pictographs etched in the weathered stones.

There might be undiscovered evidence, but I doubt it. We haven't shovel-dug very deep. The last layers of the exploratory trenches date back more than a hundred thousand years.

Habitable worlds are few, but we've found enough. If planetary life codes—amino acids, properly folded proteins, DNA, RNA, aren't close, compatible matches, we won't survive, flourish, or propagate there. If all goes well, we'll list this planet as move-in ready.

Everyone calls it The Project. It's easier to digest, to get your head around, than *Expanded Proliferation Disbursement in Layered Continuums Initiative*—not even a decent acronym. I remember when I first learned of the Dayton-Resnik Paradox. After understanding the physicist's math, scientists devised means to access the layer and branches, giving engineers the tools to build machines for travel to other realities past. The ripples carry you to a branched timeline without disturbing your personal one. You can't go back to kill your grandparents before they met.

Some propose the effect is a piercing into alternate universes, but the math doesn't support it—there's a distinct difference between the two; moving to an alternate universe, if they exist, would take as much energy as contained in hundreds of supermassive black holes, perhaps more. We can branch-jump time layers by sipping energy drawn from the quantum vacuum.

In the two hundred years of The Project, we've found no technologically intelligent, let alone human, life. The stars and galaxies we see today are in the right places for the time jump. Though younger, by about fifty thousand to several million years, not much in cosmic time.

Fifty thousand is the closest we can jump from our time. Attempts to go back to more recent times always fail. The physicists insist it isn't a barrier per se, but the nearest point on the other side of the hump we have to jump over—their way of dumbing it down for us. We call it the sweet spot. Far enough back for things to be cosmically similar and close enough for our purpose—prevent the inevitable extinction of our species by seeding timelines with regressed stock.

Leaning forward toward land, I envision the first settlers here walking along the shore. A hardy, robust group, physically and mentally designed for natural hardship and competitive breeding, survival of the fittest, with environmental pressures improving the species. A thing long lost to our timeline. We have weeded our genetic garden too much and removed too many variances, thinking them weak spots.

A reversible syndrome, but unpalatable to most—we've become too comfortable, too civilized, and uniform. In conquering and controlling everything, we've conquered ourselves to the point of not wanting to share our timeline.

Nature doesn't like that, preferring constant change and competition. The first colony here will start from ground zero. They'd have primitive skills and knowledge to survive and to build but not much else beyond simple tools and fire. If they take hold, and even if they don't, other colonies, years from now, will be planted far away on other continents. We'll leave the ship here, stocked with essentials and raw materials.

Eight hours before our time here is up. I've gathered the fifteen surveyors still aboard—one three-person team is still in the field. "Before we go back, let's hear a synopsis of each group's data. Geology?" It isn't necessary, but it has filled some time, tamping idle, individual thoughts about staying.

Sandra Fencil stands in the low-ceilinged second deck, which serves as our living and research area. "Tectonics present, but no indications of any meaningful catastrophic events for at least seven to twelve thousand years from now, very stable. Magnetosphere, same thing. The core is still young, hot, and rotating. There's evidence of volcanism in this area, but long since subsided. The hot spots have drifted to the south."

"Questions?" I ask. There are none. It's a rehash of what we learned from the probes, verified by our eyeball observations. I know she has more but wants to run a definitive analysis back at the Project labs before offering any amplification to the bare-bone facts.

"Biology, you're up next." Jefferson, our resident curmudgeon, starts his banter.

"This is the most compatible world we've yet to find. No bio-forms we can't acclimate the settlers to. Predation is limited mostly to smaller forms that skitter away from us. The Goosers aren't hostile unless you get close to their broods. All the larger land mammals are herbivores, except for what we've called the Carno-cats... those help maintain a balance in the larger fauna populations."

"Agronomy?"

"Several native grass and tuber species seem to have regressed from a cultivated stock—you can tell by the distribution patterns." Yanich stays seated. He isn't one to spend energy without good cause unless gathering samples. "Future seed selections should create larger grain and root sizes within three generations. The sea plant growths show an inordinate uptake of heavy metals, which isn't critical as it acts as a purification media. Not edible, though. And I wouldn't eat the marine life that dines on it."

"Archeology, Udahl?"

"Only the expected bones of current species. Though there was a thinning out of larger mammal species about fourteen thousand years ago—the reason is unknown until we get the soil cores back for examination. It might have been biological or some impact disaster. Pottery shards in the upper layers, but again, we don't know for sure yet; everything's so fragmented, and we don't have the proper equipment here to validate it."

"Okay, is everyone ready for the trip back? Let's get things stowed. Make it neat for the colonists." I receive assenting nods from the group leaders. "As soon as Devon and his team get back, we'll be on our way."

We'll be on our way even if he doesn't get back. We pre-set the return time before coming here. There's no button to push.

* * *

Devon halts his team. "This is as far as we go. Nothing new. Samantha, ease that rock back in place. No point in looking at the bottom of another stone. We need to get back."

Samantha releases her long pry-bar, and the rectangular stone, partially excavated, falls back into its hole with a thud, its carved bottom, unseen, unread, reverse imprinting the soil beneath it: *Coliseum aurea per stadia doudecim* — Coliseum, twelve stadia.

THE GHOST AND THE MACHINE
CHRISTINA ENGELA

Christina Engela is a South African editor and author of horror, fantasy, and science fiction novels. Her books are never short of suspense, adventure and humor, while her colorful characters and thought-provoking settings take readers into another world, making her one of the most gifted and creative story-tellers. A firm supporter of the LGBT community, Christina believes that sexual and gender minority characters aren't reflected enough by authors due to a number of reasons. As such, Christina's writing isn't stereotypical, and her characters aren't stereotypes, regardless of their sexuality or gender.

At fifty-seven years, Professor Albert Nimitz had always been a mild-mannered sort—a quiet, lanky, dedicated, academic type who wore glasses and preferred golf shirts rather than the more popular and comfortable tee. Although he'd been a card-carrying MENSA member for most of his life, he never mentioned it in conversation since he felt it was pretentious to do so, and bringing it up always made him feel somehow arrogant.

Albert despised elitism, particularly among scientists. Science, in his view, had a far more important role to fulfill than to garner one man a few accolades or to attract envious faux admiration from colleagues who—for most of his career— had done nothing but compete with him or had worked for years to sabotage his research.

No, in Albert's view, science existed to make the world better for *all* who lived on this crowded, fading Earth.

For the past nearly two decades, Professor Nimitz had worked in a physics laboratory suite belonging to a local university, and for all that time, he'd relied on sponsorships, grants, and donations from government and a few corporations, as well as academic institutions to keep his research on the go.

Albert had never married or had children, nor were there— lingering at the back of his mind—any vain hopes that one day, someone in their mid-thirties would knock on his door, looking for their daddy. No—he'd always scoffed and shrugged off all the goading and questioning from friends and relatives about when he was to find the right girl, get married, and raise a family.

"Bringing a child into *this* world would be a despicable act of child abuse!" Was something he often said, in true cynical fashion. The right girl, he scoffed—he'd *already* married the right girl—and her name was Science.

Still, he wasn't a cynic—not truly. Yes, it had been a lonely life—and to avoid thinking about that too much, Albert kept himself busy with knotty mathematical problems, solving the latest challenges to his research and development. In all that time spent toiling in the lab, the only person to keep him company was his research assistant Dr. Gary Myers, a man eleven years his junior, who had a string of PHDs and honors as—well, *almost* as long as his own. Gary shared Albert's vision—and his passion.

All that struggling was about to pay off now, at last—

finally! It had taken nearly eight years to finalize everything on paper—carefully annotated in a series of old-school, black-covered, paper notebooks, jotted down from countless frenzied whiteboard scribble sessions—lovingly typed into a succession of desktop PCs and eventually, laptops. The software simulation phase was supposed to have taken another two years after that, but funding cuts and difficulties experienced in finding a suitable software guru at the time resulted in that part of the project overshooting the mark by three years. Finally, Albert's project entered the practical test phase, with the construction of numerous small-scale test beds and prototypes—with the first working small-scale prototype, delivering a successful outcome only the previous year.

Of course, success had come at a price—a rather messy one in the form of several bins of dead rats, some of which had gone into the device at one end, vanished—and reappeared on the other end, not looking quite... well, like rats. Worse still—seemingly—others had simply disappeared into the machine, never to be seen again. Where they ended up, Professor Nimitz had no idea—but one thing was sure, wherever they were, the answer probably included the word *'quantum'* in it somewhere.

Still, even the dean—a man who'd considered the project *'a hopeless waste of time and resources'*—seemed impressed, admitted that Nimitz was *'onto something,'* and scuttled off to approve a check for the next phase of the project: a life-size machine that could do the same thing to actual human beings.

Professor Nimitz fervently hoped *'the same thing'* meant transporting humans from one device at one end of the lab, to another at the other end—intact and not missing or inverted like some of the earlier rats. Of course, it had been some months since that had last happened—over two years—in fact, almost all of the last hundred or so most recent test subjects who'd been put through the machine sat quietly in their cages in the next room, largely undisturbed by the fact every molecule in their little bodies had been dematerialized, broken up, digitized into a signal, transmitted, received, reassembled, and rematerialized again. Some of them even up to ten times—with no noticed ill effect. They were still rats after all and alive.

Albert Nimitz was almost beside himself with excitement. What they had here—what they were on the edge of—was the realization of his dream: a transmatter device! A machine that could transmit matter. It would revolutionize global transportation and cut down the use of fossil fuels, not to mention cut down risks of accidents while traveling by road, rail, sea, or air. Airlines might buckle, he mused, oil companies implode —but the world would be better for it.

Instead of using those old, risky, messy, labor and time-consuming methods of transport, people could travel almost instantaneously to anywhere on the planet… his mind raced—why limit themselves? Bigger versions of his machine might transport more than one person at a time—tens, even hundreds—and perhaps even cargo too.

A receiver-transmitter unit like these full-sized prototypes could be delivered to the Moon or to Mars—or anywhere in range. Why, in the not-too-distant future, people might even have one of these in their homes—and people could dial up their destinations and travel from here to there in the blink of an eye! Fast. Safe. Intact.

It all started right here! he thought proudly—his eyes caressing the lines of the actual Transmatter Portal Model 7 like another, more carnal man's hands might caress the curves of a woman he worshipped. Across the room that was his laboratory stood another just like it—identical. Today was the big day—the day they put a test subject… an actual human being through it. As with most things in science, hopefully, everything would work out just fine.

"Ready, Professor," Gary Myers called.

"Implement," Albert said, nodding.

The transmatter was activated from the control desk which

stood in the center of the room, between the two units—with both being linked together in sync. When one was activated, the other was as well, remotely. Both units consisted of low metal-cased platforms on the floor, with what appeared to be vacant metallic door frames mounted upright on top of them. Cables and wires snaked across the floor like strands of a rat's nest. In a flash, a thin plasma-like film appeared in first one doorway, then the other, and both stabilized and remained visible.

First, the safety test. Albert certainly didn't want someone to walk through the first doorway and just disappear—but, considering the state of the first rat that had emerged from the test platform several years earlier—in an inverted state— 'disappeared' seemed marginally preferable. Preliminary testing of the new prototype had already been done in the previous week—a variety of objects had been sent through it—books, a laptop, a pot plant, and of course, a number of rats and a beagle or two. So far, not one single mishap—but today of all days, he wanted to be certain.

"Test One," he announced loudly for the watching cameras around the room and tossed a rubber ball through the opening of the first doorway. The ball vanished in mid-air as it entered, and then instantly appeared in the other doorway across the room, landed on the tiles of the floor, then bounced away.

"Success," Myers beamed.

"Test Two," Professor Nimitz announced and took a cage full of white rats off a nearby stand, placed them on the platform, and pressed it through the opening with a stick. The cage reappeared on the other side, complete with its unimpressed contents.

"Success," Myers reported again, for the cameras. "Right—ready, Professor?"

"Absolutely." Albert grinned at him, readying himself at the opening of the first doorway—eyeing the slightly opaque, filmy plasma barrier with mixed feelings of anticipation and abject terror. "Test Three!" he announced and, anticipating victory, stepped through.

Everything went black.

When Professor Albert Nimitz came to, he appeared to be looking at the room from a slightly different perspective. He also felt decidedly odd... sort of *floaty*... if that was the right word? Looking around, he noticed he was standing on the destination platform, having just exited the doorway... except... that was *another* him... he seemed to be looking at his own self from outside. It was him—right down to his glasses and greying hair... and that side-parting.

The *other* him seemed momentarily flustered, reached out for a railing to steady himself, then recovered.

"Are you all right, Professor?" Myers asked, concerned.

"I... don't know," Albert said aloud, but the *other* him had also spoken at the same time and drowned him out.

"Perfect." The impostor smiled, giving Myers a thumb's up.

"Success," Myers reported. "Well done, Professor."

"Success?" Albert protested, almost sounding like a whining dog. "Hang on a moment. I wouldn't call *this* a success!"

Regardless, the other two carried on as though he hadn't been heard.

"Hey!" he shouted, confused, angry, and frustrated all at once. "What am I—invisible? Hello! Can you hear me?"

Disturbed on several different levels, Albert walked towards the impostor, meaning to reach out and grab his shoulder—but the other figure suddenly turned and walked right into him. With a horrible shock, Albert realized that the impostor had walked right *through* him.

But... he thought, fighting a rising panic, *that's impossible!*

"Improbable," a built-in scientific sounding voice remarked in his subconscious—it had been pounded into his subcon-

scious through years of scientific practice—but, determinedly, he shook it off again. This *was* impossible.

As though to test the theory rapidly forming in his mind, Albert reached out for the nearest stand and tried to touch it— his hand passed right through it.

Mystified, he noticed that neither Myers nor the other him were reacting to him and seemed to be celebrating the apparent success of his project. Myers had cracked open a bottle of champers, and *he* was preparing the glasses, wiping them with a clean bit of rag.

Albert rested his head in one hand—the palm against his forehead felt solid and real enough. What the hell was going on? Was he dead? Was he a ghost? Albert sighed. He didn't believe in ghosts—or at least, hadn't. *Perhaps*, he thought, *it was time to reevaluate that outlook.*

On the other hand, Albert reasoned, leaning against a wall nearest the pair of celebrating scientists, *his body seemed to be quite alive and enjoying a glass of bubbly with Myers*—and he was pretty sure ghosts came from dead people—while their bodies typically played dead. Was he perhaps in another dimension? Had his machine been slightly flawed—sending him here to some parallel dimension instead of through the other side of the doorway? He shivered at the thought of erroneous calculations.

"Perish the thought!" he muttered. Of course, he couldn't entirely discount the possibility that he might have sent himself to some dimension similar to his own—one where he might arrive in a kind of incorporeal state... but he highly doubted it. Almost as if to bolster his opinion on the matter, Albert observed his disconnected and somewhat animated physical body behave quite unlike himself.

It began with a glassy-eyed sort of look in Professor's eyes, and a couple of odd little facial tics... a kind of creepy awakening.

"Professor?" Myers asked, sounding concerned. First, the

impostor turned off the cameras. Then Albert watched, shocked, as his body rudely reached out and snatched away the half-empty bottle from a surprised Myers—then smacked it hard across the assistant's face, splashing liquor across the floor. Myers cried out, stumbling backward against the control desk, putting his hands out in self-defense.

"Professor, stop—what're you doing?" Myers cried. A second blow knocked his glasses flying, where they landed, bent, on the floor some feet away. After the third blow with the heavy glass bottle, Gary Myers fell to the floor wide-eyed and groaning, blood dripping and splashing with each successive, merciless blow that rained down.

"What have you done?" Albert cried, aghast, going completely unheard. *"What have you done?"*

As the apparition given flesh and form—*Albert's*—straightened up from over the shattered body of the late Dr. Myers, Albert shuddered. He'd never seen his face pulled quite like that before, distorted into a mirthful, fascinated, cruel mask, and the sight of it shook him. The sight of poor, pitiful Myers, lying sprawled between the two control desks, head smashed in, and covered in his own blood, gave him a case of chills.

He continued watching with morbid curiosity as his own body turned the devices back on, adjusted the settings slightly so as to throw them off kilter, and dragged his late research assistant towards the first doorway.

Suddenly, "Oh, my!" said the ghost of Myers, still dressed in his bloody, mussed-up lab coat, now standing beside Albert. "What's going on? Oh… am I dead?"

Under normal circumstances, Professor Nimitz's eyes might have been a good deal wider but considering what he'd just witnessed, the sight of a deceased colleague standing beside him and talking to him seemed a slight bit tame and underwhelming.

"Seems so." He nodded in agreement.

"Oh, yes," Myers chirped, smiling in an unsettling, yet

cheery way given the circumstances, and looking down at the floor again. "I must be—can't see my feet. That's a sure sign."

Albert risked a peek down at the floor to see what Myers was talking about. He saw Myer' feet—they were there all right... it was his *own* that seemed absent. He suddenly felt queasy.

"You okay, Prof?" Myers asked. "Why'd you do it anyway? Kill me, I mean? What'd I ever do to you?"

"I didn't," Albert argued, pointing at his elderly lanky body as it struggled with the macabre task of disposing of the evidence. "He—*that*—did it! I've been stuck here like *this* since I walked through the portal."

Myers grew visibly sad as his mortal remains disappeared through the portal—and nothing came out the other side.

"That's really quite clever," Myers remarked with an audible note of admiration evident. "Mussed up the settings so the quantum phase shift is off, and anything dropped in vanishes for good... like all those poor creatures we lost."

"Yes." Albert nodded more calmly than he actually felt. The sight of a white bunny rabbit lolloping by his feet, apparently unseen by the only actual living creature in the room, served to slightly loosen his grip on reality. He persevered... "And it presents another problem—or rather *another* aspect to the same problem... I originally assumed that I'd dropped into another dimension when I arrived on the other side of the gate... instead—given the evidence..."

"What evidence, Professor?" Myers asked, studying him in a disturbing sort of way. Albert noticed his head had a little misshapen look to it as a result of the savage blows. He winced.

"Er, given the fact of your existence... in the face of the obvious," Albert said, pointing at the mess, "it seems I've simply been disembodied—in effect, I'm as dead as you... a *ghost*... a spirit—only thing is, unlike yours, my body is still quite alive... and monstrously so."

"I'm afraid so," Myers observed, as the *other* Professor Nimitz methodically cleaned up the blood smears from the floor and furnishings, whistling a cheerful, yet soulless little tune to break the silence. Nimitz found the grin on his former face and the hard, mean look in his former eyes chilling. Barren. Devoid of any warmth or humanity. It was positively nightmarish. Whatever was running the automaton, it wasn't him.

"I'm coming for you," the automaton cried with seething anger. "I'm going to get all you jealous, sabotaging sons of bitches!"

Albert suddenly understood its motives and felt a swell of pity for any of his colleagues still in the building... or perhaps even in the same zip code.

What had gone wrong? What flaw had there been in his calculations? He'd taken *everything* into account. *Everything?* Hadn't he? Well... everything he could think of—that is, everything the last almost twenty years' worth of testing, calculating, research, and experimentation had prepared him to think of.

Nimitz's device broke down physical matter and even the energy in devices, dematerialized and transmitted them to a receiver, which reassembled everything as it had been... animals had gone through the device, as had electronic tools like mobile phones—and the last experiments had shown promising results, with no discernable changes in structure. The phones retained their electric charges. The test animals' behaviors remained consistent... of course, one couldn't ask a rat in a cage questions and expect an answer, could one? Besides, a lab rat might harbor feelings of extreme resentment towards lab-coated humans—and with good reason.

No, Albert surmised, the machine had reassembled everything perfectly—atoms, cells, muscles, organs, and tissues—all except for one thing—something which the machine hadn't accounted for... something the machine never knew was there.

How could he have programmed the machine to account for something he himself had never believed existed?

Albert rallied and scoffed at the thought, then relented as the truth—the cold, hard facts of the matter became apparent. As he and Myers impotently watched the other Albert discard his lab coat by the door on its way out—pausing to lift the fire axe from its mounting onto his shoulder, Albert couldn't deny the obvious anymore. Somehow, that indefinable spark which had made Albert Nimitz, *Albert Nimitz* had been left out of the final assembly, discounted, omitted, discarded.

His soul.

ANGELIC

DAVID BOOKER

David Booker is originally from Chicago Illinois but after twenty-four years in the U.S. Air Force, he retired as a master sergeant in Beavercreek, OH. His love of history led him to write the Time Is *series of time travel novels. He has also completed two books of short stories under the title of* A Glimpse of My Shorts. *In these, he has written a collection ranging from horror, humor, science fiction, rants, and raves. He has a YouTube Channel where he reads from his books, as well as those of his friends.*

George's pack pressed heavily on his back, pinning him down. He frantically tried to raise himself from the muddy water. Bubbles rose to the surface as he strove to heave himself up. Realizing he was handling the situation wrong, he raised one arm and bent his leg. Slowly, he pushed. With effort, he was able to raise his head above the cold muddy water. Locking his arm, he rested. With another concerted effort, he slid his leg up further and pressed off. Reaching a point of equilibrium, he pushed a bit harder, and the weight of his pack drew him further backwards. With shaking hands, he undid the hasps and slid his arms out of the straps.

Fiddling around in a side pocket of his duffel, his fingers grasped a small mag light. Aiming the beam at what he tripped over, he saw a long bluish black pipe-like object. He grasped it to haul it out of the path and got a surprise when he realized it wasn't a pipe but a leg. Aiming his light higher, he made out the form of an individual dressed in what looked like a motorcycle racing suit. He grasped the hand, and its glove slid off. The hand was odd, the fingers seemed long, graceful, and almost translucent.

He touched them, and the warmth informed him; this person was still alive. He tried to raise the visor without success but when he shined his beam inside the helmet, he saw a face that stopped his heart. He'd heard the term *ethereal* but until now, he'd never seen it in person. This face was beautiful. More so than he'd ever have dreamt one could be. This couldn't have been born of earth. Gazing upward, he saw the lip of a cliff and at its edge was an elm tree. He looked around and saw on the ground a light depression indicating where this body had fallen. He assumed that somewhere on that ledge was whatever vessel she had travelled in.

He tried to reassure this person that he wouldn't hurt her but would try to bring her back to her ship. Untying a collapsible stretcher from the side of his duffel, he raised her on one side. Speaking words of comfort as he laid the stretcher behind her and carefully rolled her onto it, he quickly did up the straps. Weaving a line through the grips, he took the loose end and tied it onto a stone. Bringing out a slingshot, he aimed for an overhanging branch and grinned as his first shot went soaring. Following its path as it shot, flying in a graceful arc over the branch, it landed with a thud at his feet.

"You've still got it, kid." He chuckled as he carefully and slowly pulled the stretcher up until it was level with the tree trunk's midpoint.

He tied off the end on a branch, using an intricate knot that he was confident wouldn't unravel. He tied another cord to his pack and stuffed the other end into his pocket. Using the roots that protruded from the side of the cliff, he exhaled and began his arduous climb up. Gasping at the summit, he dragged his leg over the side and breathed heavily.

Rolling onto his back, he saw the stretcher in the tree, slowly swinging in a light breeze. He braced his foot on a convenient rock and brought up his pack. In that pack was everything he possessed, and he wasn't taking any chances on losing any of it. He cut the cord holding the stretcher and carefully lowered it onto the ground. A flash of light in the helmet showed the face, eyes closed. She may have been in too much pain and passed out. He easily strapped the stretcher to his back. This person he was carrying couldn't have weighed even a hundred pounds.

He dragged his duffel over the thick grass towards an unusual craft. It was larger than he had anticipated and seemed two storied. Approaching cautiously and calling out, he waited to see if anyone would open. No response. He turned around, wondering how to proceed. As the form he was carrying faced towards the ship's side, there was a soft shush. He turned again to find a door had formed and opened. George tossed in his duffel and then bent low to clear the door. A short scan from the ship played over himself and the stretcher. The interior darkened. A line of lights formed a single path down a hallway. He followed as they lit one after another, while those behind dimmed and turned off. In the distance, he heard the ship's door close and seal.

He was led to what he took to be a medical bed. The light turned on inside. He slipped off the stretcher and laid it down gently. Carefully undoing the straps, he raised her body and laid it reverently on a mat. He tried to close the lid. It remained obstinately open. A light with the image of a person in a space suit glowed on an inside panel. Slowly, the suit faded out and only the person remained; this was repeated several times.

"Guess I'm supposed to take the outfit off of you," he mused.

He removed her helmet and placed it on a hook. Without its hindrance, his eyes gazed on a most elegant and beautiful face. He blushed at the thought of exposing this person. Looking around, he found a blanket and covered her.

Working by touch only, and that very carefully, so as not to offend, he removed the spacesuit piece by piece. The machine seemed to take no regard of the covering and allowed the thin blanket to remain. The lid closed, and another scan explored her injuries. A countdown timer which he couldn't read began, and it seemed the work of healing started.

The room darkened, and another set of lights guided him to a small lounging room. He wandered, curiously considering the things that seemed familiar though somehow altered. It was like Alice in the looking glass where objects were just close enough for him to recognize but foreign enough to be disquieting.

As George passed a panel on the wall, a door formed, and a small closet area opened. George tossed his duffel in and pulled out a cot and sleeping bag. From another partition, he found an inflatable pillow. Now that he had quarters for the night, he relaxed somewhat.

From his duffel, he pulled out a can of ravioli and popped the top. Eating so as not to spill any, he took his time over the small can, out of consideration for his hostess. When he was done, he wrapped the remains and put it in an outside duffel pocket.

Time dragged as the minutes turned to hours. He lay on his cot and tried to sleep. The reminiscent sight of that woman blotted out all other thoughts. He saw her face in his mind, chiseled by a master's hand. Even De Vinci himself couldn't capture such angelic beauty. Her form, from what he could see outlined under the blanket, was equally seraphic, and it filled his senses with rapture.

George woke by a soft light and cool breeze as the door to his closet opened, and the woman he had been dreaming of stood before him. She beckoned him out and sat him down on a pillowed chair.

Holding a wand in front of her, she spoke in a flute-like tone which was translated into English.

"Forgive me for the Brzzzt I have put you to. The ship is automated and when you brought me through, it left your planet as Brzzzt instructed. I am Brzzzt for the Brzzzt of myself. If you will return to the room you have set up as a Brzzzt, I will make arrangements for your Brzzzt."

With a warm smile, George rose, bowed, and walked into the sleeping closet. He thought of the time he would spend in this incredible ship with an angel. The door closed softly behind him. He lay on the cot with a grin. He considered that with time and effort, communication between them would become more coherent. Beyond the door, the angel went into a side room and sat at her desk. In front of her laid a panel with buttons and lights that she contemplated. With a slight shrug of her shoulders, she reached a long, graceful finger towards one of the buttons. A light was extinguished. She bent forward to look out the window to see George as he glided past it. He had a very surprised look frozen on his face. Next came floating the cot and duffel. The angelic being smiled warmly and made her way to her kitchen for something to eat.

I, MAC

CHRISTINA ENGELA

Dear Eric,

Got the keys to your apartment and received operating instructions for the cat (turn the tail three times (left, twice to the right) and got shown where Everything is. (You forgot to tell me what I'm supposed to feed it to.) Apparently, there's a Universal Remote somewhere as well, and that should come in handy... See you soon!

—Mac.

Eric Hawthorne put down the note as he finished reading it. Where was the idiot who wrote the note—Mac? Mac *who?* He didn't know anybody called Mac.

He was a bit miffed—feeling slightly puzzled. Currently sitting in the middle of his apartment, apparently, on a couch —his couch. A cat came in silently and froze as it saw him. It stood there, eyeing him with its glowing green eyes. What did this Mac mean, 'operating instructions?' How on Mars did one *operate* a cat?

It blinked at him and mewed softly. Turn the tail three times to the right and twice to the left? If he had to try that—cranking the tabby's tail—well, he had a pretty good idea the cat would object! He'd probably end up needing first aid for one thing. What was it, some kind of safe combination? And what the blazes was the Universal Remote for? The cat perhaps?

Hmm. Eric thought about that a minute more. Then again, everybody everywhere knows at least one person called Mac. (Mac Tavish or Donald or Farlane or Mac-something-or-other.) The only Mac Eric knew was a chubby, middle-aged, balding man who tended to smell of cheese mostly, sometimes onions. That Mac was an insurance salesman who worked for New Mutual ISU on Io Station. Like most people who worked there for any length of time, the Mac Eric knew had a pale complexion scornfully referred to (by people who lived on atmospheric planets) as a moon-tan. Eric was sure it wasn't *that* Mac, specifically. That Mac was still on Io station. Well, he was when Eric left there two days ago.

He'd arrived back from the space port that morning after receiving the strange note in his email while on a business trip to Io Station... And now he was back here, wondering what it was all about. For one thing, Eric wondered where the damned cat had come from. He never had a cat before. At least, he didn't when he left four weeks earlier. Cats didn't materialize out of thin air, did they? At least, he considered—rather worried—not without the assistance of some kind of teleportation device... Did it come with this Mac of this note? No, he thought—Mac had received um, operating instructions for it. But from whom? And where the hell was Mac now?

The creature rubbed up against his leg and purred as he absentmindedly scratched behind its ears. What the blazes was he talking about? Where Everything is? What Everything? And why was it written with a capital E? Who the Edgar Allan

Poe had given anyone the key to his apartment? And showed him where this 'Everything' was

The apartment wasn't the way Eric had left it. It looked like it had been lived in while he'd been away. It had a smell in it he didn't recognize and at first, he gave the cat a few suspicious glances. But soon, it seemed to him it was some kind of... perfume—aftershave, maybe? He reached down and picked up the cat. It vibrated as it purred. Eric turned it upside down, and around and over and over.

It just sort of sprawled as he did so, regarding at him in the same superior way cats regard everything lower than them (i.e. everything else). It was a cat all right. At least, it seemed to be. It was shedding all over his favorite sweater as if trying very hard to convince him that it was. *What the hell*, Eric thought, what did he have to lose? It wasn't his cat anyway. He set it up on his lap on all fours, holding it steady with his left hand and grasped its tail with his right.

The cat just stood there, giving him a disdainful sort of look as Eric cranked its tail. Okay. Three times to the left, two times to the right. The cat meowed. And that was all. Feeling like an absolute fruit loop, Eric let the cat go, apologized to it, and decided to go fetch a drink—just as the front door clicked open.

A cold chill went through his body as he realized he was probably completely defenseless and had no idea what would walk in to the room. Other than maybe harsh language, he had nothing to throw at any potential assailant. Well, okay—he could try throwing the cat at him as a sort of insane diversion —if he could still catch it in time. Eric quickly grabbed the nearest heavy object instead and shoved it behind his back under a cushion. It was, technically, man's best friend—a porcelain dog, in the—er... seated position. But it *was* heavy and had a rather pointed snout which he thought could come in handy if things went sour.

A stout male figure entered, staggering backwards under

the weight of two swollen suitcases, one in each hand. The man turned round and froze when he saw Eric sitting there. Eric gawked. It was Elvis, his cousin, Elvis Sloane! It had been *years* since he last laid eyes on his least favorite cousin, at his uncle's home in Mars City! Decades in fact (it had taken Elvis that long to recover).

Eric had many unpleasant childhood memories—the hours of torture at the hands of his elder cousins Elvis and Yuri. There was the incident with the plastic cricket bat and their favorite pastime, which consisted of swinging him around by the feet until he threw up. They called him their *'little lawn sprinkler.'* He'd been only five at the time. It had taken him years to get over it—and he still hated heights because of those monsters!

His uncle would add injury to insult and spank him because he'd ripped up the lawn with his fingers in panic while trying to get away from Elvis and Yuri. Eric's grip on the porcelain snout behind his back tightened and not altogether involuntarily either. Cousin Elvis grinned and dropped the suitcases on the carpeted floor with a single leaden thud.

"Cousin!" Elvis cried, throwing his arms open wide in a greeting that was way too familiar—and far too friendly for Eric's liking. Eric edged away as Elivs approached, calling, "How goes it?"

"Um, hello," Eric ventured, reluctantly letting go of the porcelain dog. There was no sign of Yuri, fortunately. The older of the two had always been the meaner, tougher one. Yuri and Elvis just tended to play little mister innocent, and little Eric always got the blame—and smacks from Uncle John for being 'pedantic.' Their respective parents had arguments about their 'brat son Eric.' Oh yes, it had always been pinned on him—all Eric's fault, every time.

Still in a bit of shock, "What the hell are you doing here?" Eric asked, rising.

"Just thought I'd come catch up on old times with my favorite cousin!" Elvis smiled, almost innocently.

"No, I meant it," said Eric. "What the *hell* are you doing here? And for that matter, I think you meant favorite *target*, didn't you? Like that time with the cricket bat, remember?"

"You can't still be mad about that!" said Elvis, "Surely not?" Seemingly a little taken aback. "Can't even see a scar on you!" he added, squinting as though examining Eric's face. "All nicely healed up!"

"Never mind that!" Eric snarled. "Who's this *Mac* character in the note anyway—and who the hell let you into my apartment?"

"That's me!" Elvis smiled maddeningly. *"I'm* Mac. I got the key from the floor manager!"

Blasted floor manager—Eric would have to have a talk with him later!

"No, you're Elvis!" Eric said. "Elvis Sloane! I know you are because you're the smarmy little bastard who tormented me —I still have nightmares about you! I still see your face before me as clear as day! That's you all right—Elvis!"

"Yes," said Elvis Sloan. "But people call me Mac because I'm a Mac-anic."

"A—*mac-anic?"* Eric repeated slowly, puzzled. "Sure you don't mean *maniac?"*

"No, I mean mac-anic!" said Mac with visibly mounting irritation. "Someone who fixes things!"

"Well, you fixed me all right!" Eric exclaimed exasperatedly. "Whammo—twenty stitches across the forehead—so I can believe that."

Elvis shrugged dismissively. "We were just kids!" Elvis starting his slow, inevitable approach towards Eric. "I was only nine!" Eric, feeling a little crowded, edged backwards towards the sofa.

"That's the point, you sick bastard—I was only five years

old! You were a homicidal bloody maniac! And a pathological liar—your dad hit *me* every time *you* did something wrong!"

"It was an accident."

"Yes, I know—you didn't mean to actually break the bat!"

"You're a tough nut to crack, aren't you?" Elvis persevered, smiling in a reality-denying and forcibly reconciliatory fashion.

"Apparently not—hello—twenty stitches, remember? And a concussion!"

"Well, that's all in the past now, isn't it? Come on, let's put it behind us…" Elvis said and extended a hand, still closing in on Eric. Eric hurriedly backed away. He wasn't still afraid of Elvis; that was long ago—but it could be said of him—Eric begrudgingly admitted, that he had developed trust and intimacy issues along with all the other baggage Elvis and Yuri had saddled him with—and he was damned if he would shake hands with the man.

Anyway, Eric weighed all of ninety-eight kilograms as of last Sunday, so he had his doubts about Elvis being able to swing him around now. Besides, Elvis was about forty years old already—and judging by his build, probably wasn't up to such a task anymore either.

On the other hand, if he were wrong about that, Eric's apartment might just need a new coat of paint later. In which case, he might as well pick a color now to save time. *Orange*, he thought randomly. Orange seemed nice.

"Could hear bells ringing for weeks!" Eric muttered on the verge of hysteria, still backing away from the encroaching Elvis. Eric felt the backs of his calves reach the couch, and he flumped down into it in an undignified manner. The undeterred Elvis appeared set on following through, perhaps to pluck Eric back to his feet again—and Eric's fingers instinctively closed around the porcelain dog under the cushions… and before he realized what was happening—*crash!*

Elvis Sloane stopped dead in his tracks, frozen in that

surreal, shocking instant. His eyes went squint and seemed to stare at each other with mute surprise for what seemed to Eric to be quite a long moment, before he collapsed backwards with a muffled carpetty noise.

In the suddenly deafening silence, Eric Hawthorne stared down at the badly dressed mound of family genes laying at his feet. Then at the smashed remains of the porcelain dog that laid scattered on the carpet—and the largest remaining piece in his right hand. He was rather sad about the porcelain dog—it had been given to him as a gift by a favorite aunt—on the *other* side of the family. All that was left was the snout. He meant the dog, not the aunt.

With his mind suddenly racing with blind panic, Eric looked around madly. The cat, who had been lying sleeping on the kitchen counter, raised its head, beheld the mayhem that had just played out before it, yawned as though to give the show a negative, disapproving rating, and then turned over to continue sleeping. Eric stared at the broken ceramic snout in his hand again. His knuckles were peculiarly white, he noticed, squeezing the object as panic took hold.

I've killed him! he thought, shocked and uncertain whether he should burst into tears, update his will, or roll on the floor, laughing. But this mounting terror soon turned to disappointment as he saw his cousin's bulbous chest rise and fall in the slow, regular pattern of one who is, obviously, not dead. Or perhaps not dead enough. At least, not according to Eric's taste.

Panicking, Eric checked for a pulse. *Idiot!* he thought. *He's breathing, isn't he?*

Then again, Eric had known so many men who breathed yet had no pulse. Or even a single warm spot on their entire bodies—like most of the bosses he'd known in his working life for instance... *Bastards!* No, there it was—slow and regular... There was no blood, other than what remained inside a perfectly sealed Elvis, who oddly enough, seemed to be smiling faintly. He moaned. *Damn him! Anyway, it was self-defense, Officer...* Eric thought in a characteristically Eric-like flat spin. *The man just came for me, and I swung and...*

"What's going on here?" A deep voice suddenly boomed from the doorway. Eric had such a fright that he jumped, the soles of his shoes lifting off the carpet nearly two full feet, while his arms flapped wildly, sending the broken snout flying across the room. The porcelain snout shattered against the kitchen wall tiles and sprayed bits of shrapnel noisily—audible even over Eric's shrill falsetto scream. *Well,* he thought in a surprising moment of clarity—at least that took care of the evidence, more or less. *Ha ha! Try getting fingerprints off that!*

Eric's shriek still fading from its traumatized hearing, the cat looked up at him with one eye open, both its ears drawn flat. It yawned again before returning to the task of ignoring everything else in general.

The source of the deep, booming voice, Eric realized, was his nosy next-door neighbor, Mrs. Parks. Mrs. Parks used to be in the Army, a long time ago, when the sight of a female form in camouflage with red badges on her sleeves was enough to send the enemies of the Terran Empire scurrying for safety. Her own side too, apparently. She was forever blaming Eric for the poor condition of her plants, which consistently seemed to prefer slow suicide rather than endure her daily reprimands.

The other tenants in general preferred to tackle twenty flights of stairs—carrying shopping bags—rather than spend two minutes alone with her in an elevator! Lucky for Eric, she was standing outside the door, talking rather harshly. He could imagine rows of frightened petunias standing stiffly to attention in a potted regiment outside her door, swaying slightly in abject terror while under close inspection. No wonder they were always so pale and wilted! They reminded Eric of her husband. Poor old Mr. Parks... They buried Henry Parks last year, back on Earth. Sense of humor failure, apparently. Quite an expensive plot of land too, land being at a premium on

Earth nowadays. Anyway, Henry was probably a lot happier there.

Recovering his wits, Eric rushed over and quietly shut the door, surprised that Mrs. Parks hadn't heard Eric's scream and come inside to see what was going on there. *What to do? What to do?* He had to get rid of Elvis—one way or another, preferably before the man woke up and asked him what the number of that hover bus was! Or worse yet, settled in to stay longer than he had already! Besides, Eric was far too busy to put up with such inconvenience! He had just cut short an important business trip to find out what this 'Mac' business was all about —only to find out that Mac was Elvis! The sooner he wrapped this up, the better! *Hmm...* An evil grin spread slowly across Eric's face.

He set to work.

His unconscious cousin smelled strongly of garlic and crotch rot. Elvis groaned as Eric stripped off his clothes. There was a slice of pizza in one jacket pocket, all gooey. *Yuck.* As Eric worked feverishly, thoughts of all his life's misfortunes spurred him on, especially as he traced those origins back to his dear Sloane cousins. *Cut a bit away here with the hacksaw. Maybe I will!* And as Eric worked, growing more determined as he did so, his grin became more and more pronounced. *Tie that end off good and solid!* "A mac-anic, eh? Fixes things, does he— well, this time, I'm going to fix him!"

Eric thought back to a time he wanted to become a fighter pilot but was too afraid of heights. Sickened at being inverted upside down to make a success of it. *A few stabs with the screwdriver! That feels good, doesn't it?! Okay, a few more times!!* After the cricket bat incident, poor little Eric would shiver uncontrollably at the mere sight of one, so obviously, a career in cricket was out of the question too.

It had taken many years, and plenty of visits to therapists, before Eric was more or less over it all. Eric had bullied by everybody—literally everybody at school, sometimes even the girls—and was even cowed by other kids who were bullied. Funny that he'd ended up selling insurance in the end, wasn't it? *Yeah. Real funny. Ha ha. Ironic.*

And how Eric hated selling insurance, peddling policies, doing follow-up visits and contract maintenance work, traveling all the time! All because of Elvis and Yuri Sloane, smirking and giggling while their father gave him another backhand for 'being pedantic'. Well, he would reward Elvis for his efforts! He'd reward him handsomely.

Maybe, Eric thought, he should've gone into law or even better, law enforcement. "Ha!" he cried aloud, then because it felt like such a cathartic release, he added, *"Ha! Ha!"*

Just wait until he met Yuri again one day. Oh, he'd fix the brute!

Then, with a final florish, *voila*—Eric's work was done. Now all he had to do was put Elvis out of his misery. Justice at last! *Ha ha ha ha!*

His eyes fell on the cat again, where it still reclined on the counter. It watched him with utter disdain, the way cats tend to do. "Some things never change," said Eric, "but *I* have! This is so liberating! I should've done this years ago! What're you looking at?" he asked the cat sarcastically.

"I," said the cat in warm, mellow tones, "am looking at a crime in progress, a small man kicking a bigger man while he's down, a genuine coward at work!" Eric went on examining his efforts, not quite registering. "Meow. Saucer of milk, please," the cat added.

"Kicking him when he's down?" Eric mused. "Didn't think of that! Thank you! What the hell, why no—"

With his leg paused mid-backswing, Eric paused—before tilting his head at a funny, puzzled angle. He lowered his foot slowly. Deliberately. Then turned. The cat sat licking its lips, looking expectantly at him.

"I'm sorry," Eric began in a shocked, little voice. "Did—did you say something?"

"I asked for a saucer of milk," said the cat, its lips actually moving in time with the words, pronouncing each syllable, before adding, "Please? Oh and I almost forgot. Meow."

"Guh—guh," Eric stammered, staring at the cat.

Flippantly, the cat quipped, "I'm sorry, I don't speak, Idiot. Try speaking louder. Or slower. Or both. It usually works for Mrs. Parks. At least, she thinks it does. At least she doesn't say things like 'here, kitty-kitty.' It's downright insulting!" The cat appeared to notice Eric's efforts and craned its neck as if to examine it closer. "Sa-ay—I like what you did, nice work! The big bow is a nice touch! But isn't pink supposed to be for girls? Silly Human conventions! And what are all the frills for? Oh yes, um—*meow!*"

"What the…" Eric stammered, exasperated, his tone and rate of speech rapidly descending into hysterical babble, "why do you keep saying 'meow'? I mean if you can actuall speak, um—silly question, you do speak… I mean, obviously… *Goddammit… bugger… damn!*"

"Why, to blend in of course, silly human! Meow. If I didn't actually say 'meow,' you would soon know I was… something else."

"Something else?" asked Eric. Now more confused and disconfuckulated than he remembered being in his whole life. "Like what? A talking cat?" He babbled to himself, "Okay, so there's this cat in my apartment I don't remember having— and my idiot nemesis cousin and personal torturer turns up and tries to embrace me. I bonk him with a *porcelain* dog, then take out a little vengeance, as you would—Now this cat starts talking and hints that it's not in fact, a cat?" Chiding internally, *Cats* don't *talk.*

Weighing the contradictory evidence of his senses, his education and hours spent surfing the interweb and volumes of cute cat videos, together with the experiences of the last few decades of his life, Eric swallowed hard before venturing a question. To the, ah—*cat.*

"So, if you're not a cat... what are you?"

"Silly human!" purred the um, cat. "Why, I'm a Catatian of course!"

"A Catatian?"

"Species 42709A from Catatia!" said the non-cat proudly. "Look it up in your Imperial Terran star charts. The star my home orbits is called the Cat's Eye. Any resemblance to the feline species, however, is purely coincidental. Meow."

"No, no—it's quite all right! Eric quavered. "I'll take your word for it!"

"My name's Catisha."

"Bless you."

"No, that's my name—Catisha."

"Oh. That's nice. I'm Eric."

"Meow."

"Oh, bugger." Eric sighed dismally, sinking into the couch and almost instantly slumping back into the little grey heap he'd been earlier. Elvis would wake up soon and want to redecorate his apartment—probably with Eric. Or his contents. And he was wasting that valuable time in having a conversation with a cat. Oh boy.

"What's the matter?" his apparently illegal alien in the form of a house cat asked. There was a noticeable pause before it again added the obligatory, "Meow. Sorry."

"T.M.I." sighed Eric.

"Sorry, wot?"

"Too Much Information." Eric huffed, "Oh, gods!" he moaned. "I have a headache."

Resigning himself to the fact that he would get arrested for attempted murder, assault, abduction, and just to add injury to insult, charged for giving refuge to an illegal alien, and making a fool of a relative, And afterwards he would be dragged away to the wah-wah farm for talking to a cat he didn't even have! The fact that it seemed to be talking back wouldn't help his case any either.

"*Hmmmirrr,*" said the cat, purring loudly. "Funny, I thought he would be the one with the headache. Heh heh. Sorry. Meow. What are you going to do with him anyway?"

"Stop it!" pleaded Eric in the throes of his own private nightmare. "I need to think a while. Think you could please *not* talk for a little while? It's very distracting."

"*Hmmirrr,*" Catisha purred, settling down to continue its snooze. So, what was Eric to do about Elvis? What indeed?

Eric pulled out his laptop and emailed a letter he'd hurriedly drafted (in Elvis' name) to his aunt and uncle, Cora and Bruce Sloane, Mars City, claiming that Eric had been very forgiving but despite this, he had been overcome by guilt and shame for the shabby treatment he had inflicted upon his cousin and felt obliged to join the Foreign Legion. As *Elvis*, he also pointed out, the minimum term of service in the Legion was either twenty years or life, whichever came first. He then had Elvis' baggage collected and sent back to Mars City, via Pluto Station—which happened to be completely in the opposite direction and on the outskirts of the solar system.

The courier agent asked him if he was sure, and Eric said, "Yes, even though it would cost me, (that is, Elvis) four times as much as a more—um, direct route."

On Elvis' behalf, Eric went to the extra expense to take out insurance on the parcels and stuck the slip under the big pink bow Catisha had mentioned. After all, Eric had charged everything to Elvis' account so it was really, *really* worth it—for Eric.

By the time the second courier arrived to collect the two large trunks in the centre of his lounge, Eric had recovered his grin again. In fact, he was on the point of giggling uncontrollably as the two large men grunted and groaned under its weight as they lifted and carried it out the door of his apartment to put it on the robo-trolley. Once more, he took out insurance and charged the whole lot to Mr. E. Sloane. As the courier guys left and their robo-trolley trundled away behind them down the passage and turned a corner, Eric delightedly slammed the door to his apartment and did a short but vigorous 'who's-yer-daddy' dance, which involved some rather embarrassing hip-swaying and stabbing his one arm into the air.

"Elvis has left the building!" Eric giggled, while pouring a glass of champagne from a big magnum bottle he'd been saving for a special occasion. Once he'd run out of steam, he threw himself onto the sofa and settled down patiently, to wait.

A short while later, back at their dispatch and processing center, the courier service realized that the trunk they had collected from number three-four-oh-two Saturn View Heights was in fact intended for number three-four-oh-*three* Saturn View Heights—and the agents said, *'oh, bugger!'* and then hauled it all the way back again. Eric spotted both of the courier agents through the door-cam screen as they passed, giving Eric's apartment door a dirty look in passing. One rang the buzzer at the delivery address, right next door, and a few moments later, the door opened.

"Ye-es?" said a deep voice from within.

"Special delivery, man—er, I mean *ma'am*," one agent said, quickly recovering, holding a computerized clipboard with one hand, and shifting a shabby peak cap backwards with the other. "Just thumbprint here for me, right thumb please."

"Sorry, I don't have a right thumb—lost it in action on Guatamalia Four, y'know!" Mrs. Parks informed him, "This one's artificial."

"Okay," the agent agreed, sounding like he wanted to be reasonable. "The left one then."

"This one's also artificial!" Mrs. Parks explained loudly, "Lost it in action as well!"

"All right then," the agent sighed, at the end of his shift as well as his patience. "Please press any… er… remaining natural appendage that bears a traceable skin imprint against this pad."

"Are you trying to be funny?" Mrs Parks boomed. "Why, in my Army days…"

"No, ma'am!" the courier quickly interjected. "Not in the least! Please—just use whatever you use on fingerprint scanners."

"Very well." Mrs Parks subsided. She reached across, held it up, and promptly pressed the tip of her nose against it. "There!"

"Thank you!" said the agent, grateful that was over with. The robo-trolley unloaded the trunk practically on her doormat beside her pot of half-dead flowers, and without further ado, the courier service shuffled off back to their depot.

Slightly surprised and somewhat bemused, Mrs. Parks eyed the trunk that had been offloaded at her doorstep. It had a big pink ribbon wrapped around it, with a large bow tied on top. A tag on the lid said in bold anonymous block-letters: 'FROM A SECRET ADMIRER.' Mrs. Parks stood there in the doorway, rubbing her hands thoughtfully while trying to decipher the origins of this… gift. Why was it so big? What could possibly have been inside?

Then, wondering how she would get this thing into her apartment on her lonesome, she momentarily regretted letting the delivery party offload it right there and not inside. Then she decided it might be lighter once she opened it and could decide further actions based on the merits of the contents. She gave the ribbon a short pull and off came the bow. Another quick tug and the latch came free. Then she lifted the wooden lid and let it fall over backward on its hinges. Underneath was a pink satin cloth. *Oh, how… interesting,* thought Mrs. Parks.

Just as she reached out to pull this item aside, it seemed to erupt outward. Whatever was under it had launched upright and was now waving appendages at her. Taken by fright, she jumped back and got a better look at her 'gift.' It was a short, tubby man, naked except for a vibrant pink satin loin cloth tied fast with pink bows and ribbons. He stood there, moaning and groaning, wide eyed and staring at the world around him in abject horror, his hairy chest heaving and grimy fingernails clawing the air.

Her eyes fell on the man's chest—somebody had written, 'Let's Get Kinky, Lovebunny' on him and drawn a big heart underneath with an arrow through it with a bright pink marker. Mrs. Parks managed quite a passable falsetto scream before her pitch descended into 'raging bull' territory. She set about performing what she later described as a 'citizen's arrest'—but as Eric watched unseen from across the passage, on the other side of his door security monitor, he decided that what had transpired could be described as a summarized reenactment of the Battle of Guatamalia about forty years previously. (A lot of good men died at Guatamalia, apparently —Eric had been watching the History Channel.)

All the neighbors on the same floor came into the corridor to see what was going on, as well as the building security staff, who had to subdue a screaming Mrs. Parks with a shock-stick to get her off a shrieking and whimpering Elvis. Two police officers arrived shortly after that and arrested the extremely puzzled man for lewd behavior and took him away for questioning, protesting all the way.

One of the cops came back a little later to take a statement from Mrs. Parks, just as the paramedics had finished giving her a once-over and some sedatives. He didn't stay for long.

Eric sat there. He kept sitting, even after it was over, watching the mayhem on his screen—and grinning. Grinning and watching and giggling. Grinning and giggling and sipping champers. Sipping champers and watching and grinning and giggling some more. Pretty soon, it became more about sipping champers and then sipping more champers. Eric even poured some into a dish for the cat and giggled when it said 'thank you,' added a fake 'meow,' and proceeded to lap it up in a convincingly cat-like manner.

By the end of the magnum, his head spinning and his lust

for vengeance very much satisfied, Eric rose from the couch and staggered off to bed, well-pleased with himself. Justice had been done!

Eric awoke sometime the following morning, feeling rested, inspired, and fresh despite the amount he had to drink the previous night. He lay there pondering the peculiar dreams he remembered from the previous night. His cousin Elvis visiting and a talking cat—and Mrs. Parks! What a combination. *Brr!* Imagine that! Must've been the snacks on the ferry from Io Station. Next time, he decided, he would stick to raisins and peanuts. What a business.

Imagine, he postulated, what if Elvis *really* came to visit? Wouldn't that be terrible? Ha! Imagine Eric *actually* putting Elvis inside a big wooden box! And the air holes, supposing they weren't enough to keep the man alive? What a mess that would've been! A warm weight on his chest he wasn't aware of before it moved suddenly and yawned in his face.

"Eeeuw!" he moaned. "I thought cat food smelled bad going in!"

The cat turned its head to look him in the eye. It looked very unimpressed. He froze. *Just a second,* he thought, *I don't have a cat. But –*"Hello?" he said.

"Meow," said the cat, convincingly. Eric relaxed again, still a little confused about where this cat had come from.

"Thank goodness!" Eric cried in utter relief. "It was all just a dream, a bloody nightmare!"

"Bad dreams?" inquired the cat, purring contentedly.

"Aaah!"

"Oow! My ears! What did you do that for?" Catisha complained, shaking its head, and jumped to the floor. "You're far too tense; you should learn to relax," it said, walking toward the bedroom door. "We should get a cat. I never had a pet before, but they say having one around helps reduce your stress levels. You'll see!"

Catisha left the bedroom while Eric kept screaming.

DINNER WITH THE DOGE
OR STAGNATION VS. DIRECTIONAL CHANGE
HOWARD LORING

A lifelong artist, Howard Loring is as actor, printmaker, painter, and sculptor, as well as the author of both novels and short stories which blend historical fiction and time travel. Married, he currently resides in the southeastern United States. He enjoys interacting with his readers and can be contacted via his Facebook fan page or his website: www.howardloring.com

---

"It's time, Hal," said the disembodied voice, seemingly uttered from nowhere. Yet it was familiar, and this was somehow comforting. Then, the sleeping man opened his eyes, suddenly remembering who he was. "Already?" Hal asked, still prone but now blinking a few times in vain hopes of focusing on something tangible in the dim room, which was currently lit only by a small corner fireplace and a few strategically dispersed candles.

"Look, you oaf, it's not yet sunrise," he then observed, casting a glance through the darkened window. Always grumpy after awakening, Hal next added, "I see no one here. Have they come to attend us, are they outside?"

"No," answered the other, while holding forth a large tankard of steaming, heavily spiced wine. "But soon enough. The uncooperative wind has finally arrived."

This got the attention of the man on the bed. He tried to sit up a few times, but these were only hasty and futile attempts. Being quite corpulent, he extended his beefy arm, wishing assistance.

"To our advantage, or theirs?" he next inquired.

"Theirs, I'm afraid," uttered the standing man. And then, he added, "You know what you must do, Hal. It must be done quickly, and you know this, also."

The man was busy downing his tankard while these words were spoken. This day, he would need his wits about him, and the warm wine would surely help. Plus, he always loved warmed, spicy wine in the morning.

"Delightful," he said, while wiping his mouth with his sleeve. Next, holding out the empty cup, he sighed and belched. The man before him, using a deep ladle, then dutifully refilled it from a large copper vessel hanging in the fireplace.

"I will not make peace with the French," suddenly barked the seated man, who still disheveled was nevertheless the current King of England. "They are in my waters uninvited, and I won't have it. I must deal with them and will."

The standing man, who now held the pissing pot, also sighed. "And they call me a fool," he said.

Once the king was well toileted and suitably attired, which took some time to accomplish, footsteps approached in the hall. It was now well past dawn. The two occupants of the starkly furnished, yet best available room in the small fortress, now stood abreast, awaiting.

Three loud knocks on the door followed, whereupon the royal sentry stationed outside opened it to reveal a half-dozen well-dressed gentlemen standing in the corridor.

"My Liege," said the Constable of Southsea Castle, bowing

with great deference. The men surrounding him quickly did likewise. "I trust Your Majesty slept well even given our crude accommodations."

The king, by chance visiting nearby Portsmouth when informed of the newly arrived French fleet, had the day before invested the diminutive outpost, one of many fortifications built to protect the large northern estuary off the Isle of Wight. The small castle's crenulated wall would give a spectacular, unobstructed view of events, and Henry, after decades of spending good money on his ever-expanding navy, wanted to see the result of this royal largesse. He therefore anticipated a good show.

"My Lords," he decreed, "I shall savor sweet sleep only when England is safe. Tell me of the wind. It now favors the enemy?"

"It does, Your Majesty," answered the realm's Secretary of State, William Paget, who stood beside the castle's constable. "The Lord High Admiral Russel, now observing from the wall above, has already dispatched some number of row barges, the only craft we currently possess that will advance without sail, to meet several French galleys that are currently probing our line. And yet, my Lord Admiral believes the wind may soon turn to our advantage, or so he says."

To this declaration, the king only grunted. Then he stepped forward, toward the men who all stepped back at his advance. But at the doorway, he turned, once more looking to his royal jester, William Sommers.

"And what will you do today, Billy?" he asked the very tall man.

"I shall travel to Venice, Hal," calmly answered his hard-working fool, "twenty-five years hence, to sup with the Doge."

The men in the hallway all laughed at this response, but King Henry did not. His Majesty knew this unique person as no one else did, and he was well aware that if the tall man truly wished to undertake such a sojourn, he certainly could.

This seemingly simple servant, the sovereign well understood, was in reality a time traveler.

"You still have an option," added the determined jester, his thin face completely devoid of emotion.

Henry's vividly dark, pinched, and beady eyes met those of his devoted companion, looking deeply into them, searching but not finding any further meaning hidden there.

"You are a fool," then answered the king but smiled as he spoke.

The day, bright and beautiful, turned long with little real action attached. The wind ever changing was always slight, and neither side did more than maneuver at some distance from one another. The row barges, never coming close enough, did not engage the enemy, who lacking propulsion simply failed to arrive.

Upon the parapet, the king and his advisors spent the opportunity eating and drinking and talking of the coming confrontation. Considering the unique nature of the still-unfolding situation, the royal functionaries had been kept to a minimum, but those on hand milled about, ready for service if need be. Many livered attendants were of course nearby, as they were always present in abundant numbers about the king's person.

There was much speculation by everyone as to what would occur once the fleets engaged, for the indecisive wind often increased but always departed, and this left plenty of idle interval to while away whilst discussing the subject.

The king's still nascent navy was tiny, much smaller than the mighty French fleet, but being from an island nation, his seamen, unlike hers, were real sailors. Other major European powers used their fleets for transporting troops and equipment to fight on land, but England's ships fought at sea and well understood its advantages. And, the navy's two principal warships were now present in the Solent, the expansive waterway betwixt the Isle of Wight and England's southern coast.

Portsea Island stood midway in the vast estuary, and Southsea Castle was located at its point. The sweeping vantage presented between the fort's crenels was indeed panoramic. By noon, the stagnated wind again picked up.

"How many French ships?" demanded the king, sensing at last a change in the stalemated status quo. He stood leaning at the wall, squinting in the distance. "More than me, that's easy to see," he added, in a regal but sour tone.

"At least two hundred, Your Majesty," answered Henry's Lord High Admiral, who stood nearby. "We have but eighty or so. Several of yours, however, are more massive," he quickly added.

This statement referred to England's two largest ocean-going craft, both of them interesting ships.

First, they were designed and constructed specifically for warfare at sea, a unique circumstance given the times. Other ships of war, in England and elsewhere, were always converted merchantmen or were built by altering the well-established designs of ocean-going commercial vessels. Yet, by intention, these two were far superior craft, being not merely transporters of men and arms, but huge, coordinated, and highly mobile, total weapon systems in themselves.

Second, after seeing long years of heavy action in two separate and brutal wars against two different but equally stubborn French kings, both ships had been successfully and painstakingly retrofitted with the latest technological innovations. These included sealing gunports amid multiple decks that employed bronze and iron cannon and demi-cannon of various sizes. Most heavy guns were now also breech loaded, and this inventive time-saving advancement granted much inherent strategic advantage.

These novel arrangements currently permitted for the first time in nautical history the use of the broadside, a practice whereby all arms a ship possessed, port or starboard, or even both, if need be, could be fired simultaneously.

This new, striking development would quite alter standard naval tactics, by setting in place unfolding changes in maritime strategy becoming preeminent for hundreds of years.

The larger of the two great ships, the Mary Rose, was literally bristling with guns, for a new complement of cannon had been installed amidships upon an added tier between the castles, which were the higher decks on either end of the carrack-style vessel. These opposing rows of artillery naturally made the gigantic boat much heavier and so increased her displacement, which meant that she sat lower in the sea. In fact, now fully manned and abundantly provisioned, her first line of gunports rode only three feet above the waterline, a detail of some importance.

"What's happening?" barked the impatient King.

His chief functionaries, who were scattered about the edge of the parapet, had no suitable response to this. None of them knew. Still, the king could not be kept waiting, so the lord admiral was soon compelled to answer.

"It appears, Your Majesty," he admitted, "the unimpressive winds have once more ceased to blow."

"Blast it," screamed Henry. "Blast it to Hades."

He turned to retake his appointed seat, a heavy chair in the near distance placed under a colorful canopy, beside an equally heavy table that bore much food and libation, but midway, there the now overly agitated king changed his mind.

Exercising the royal prerogative, he instead stomped off, gruffly announcing over his shoulder, "My Lords, I'm to my accommodations to rest my infernal leg. Send word once something definite occurs. Until then, I'm not to be disturbed."

"Majesty," and "Sire," and such were uttered by all present. Each of them bowed toward the retreating regal presence. Two gentlemen, the constable and his lieutenant, followed the king to assure his safe transit.

The hard-working fool dutifully waited to tend his sovereign's acute affliction, something he'd done many times before. The King of England had a large, pungent ulcer on his upper thigh, which for years, despite constant attempts, had stubbornly refused to mend. The ever-oozing wound was washed and redressed several times daily, a protocol of long standing that thus far had failed to achieve any suitable, permanent solution.

"Well, Billy boy, how was your visit?" asked the monarch, once his enormous leg, newly exposed, was propped across a crude wooden stool. "Have a good dinner out of your excursion, did you? Something tasty I trust, for all of your trouble."

"It was a dismal failure," the jester replied flatly. "The Doge is as hardheaded as you, I fear. But I've another invitation a week hence that will, from my point of view, take place later today, just after we're done here. Of course, from your reference, this won't happen for another twenty-five years."

He was dabbing thick green pus from Henry's thigh as he spoke. This ministration, as those that would follow was deliberate, yet slowly and gently delivered. Still, the time traveler knew such action was useless in the long term.

The royal lesion would never heal.

"What do you wish from him?" inquired the king, referring to the Doge. After all, international intrigue was Henry's life's blood. He was highly interested, for His Majesty always relished political machinations and stratagem of any kind.

"He has to stop warring with the Sultan," answered the nursing man, "as you must with the French. The time is ripe, and Europe should now turn its eyes westward, as I've told you. Your beautiful sailing ships, and those of other European powers will permit this occurrence, but only when peace comes."

"Why grant accommodation when I can win?" asked the king.

"But will you win?" countered the fool. "The French are

more numerous, and the uncooperative weather remains fickle. Yet, you still have time to alter things."

"How so?" inquired Henry.

The patient jester then washed the king's open wound, a gaping and most grisly one. The unforgiving ulcer was deeply buried within the noble but flabby flesh. Periodically, the upper layer of skin did mostly recover but, in each instance, it was only a matter of time before the gash once more violently erupted, and ever with a nasty, highly odiferous, pus dripping vengeance.

"My Lord Brandon, as we speak, is being rowed ashore," explained his fool. "He's been conferring with Admiral Dudley aboard his flagship, the Great Harry. The finalized order of attack has now been dispersed to the fleet, but the languid wind still gives you leave to countermand this proposed action."

Charles Brandon, the first Duke of Suffolk, was Henry's oldest friend, his closest advisor, and his former brother-in-law. Years ago, he had married the king's now dead sister, Mary Tudor. The great Mary Rose was named for her.

John Dudley, currently Viscount Lisle, was in command of the fleet. One day in the not-too-distant future, Lord Dudley would be invested the first Duke of Northumberland. On another day further still, Henry's oldest daughter, who was also named Mary, would execute him, after he'd tried but failed to install as queen his son's docile young wife, the very plain and overly pitiful Lady Jane Grey.

Without hesitation, Henry firmly decreed, "No, I will see this through, my dear Billy. I've no other course open to me. I cannot make peace at such a disadvantage."

The nurse began to rewrap the wound, but Henry waved him off. Again, His Majesty was most agitated. True, this was his normal demeanor, but now more so.

"Leave it," he mumbled in a distracted fashion. Then, in a louder voice, he commanded, "Let it breathe for a while."

The jester then leaned back and sat on the floor before the king. For a moment, neither man spoke. Then Henry, always wishing answers, continued his scrutiny.

"Tell me of the Doge," he requested. "Why does he not comply with your wishes? What stops him from making peace?"

The tall man rearranged himself, by wrapping his long arms around his longer legs.

"Venice will lose Cyprus in the treaty, her last Mediterranean island, a heavy price for such a proud people," answered the jester. "Yet the Doge must accept this difficult condition and will. As you do, he just needs persuading."

The King of England laughed aloud at this proclamation. No one ever told him what to do or lasted long after such a brazen affront. No one but his fool, that is.

"And how will you change him?" Henry then asked.

"I shall take a different dinner guest with me," was the answer. "The one I took this morning was unimpressive, as I've said. Still, given that the groundwork is now sufficiently laid, my new companion should nicely do the trick."

Henry, adjusting his great bulk in the chair, then grunted.

"Who did you take?" he wondered.

"I thought the Doge needed a framework," was the reply, "a tangible yet palatable argument for making peace with the dreaded Turk, the horrid infidel. For this reason, I took the much-revered fourth century Bishop of Hippo, for he has swayed millions having such concerns. Yet, the Doge was unmoved."

"What's that you say?" demanded the now startled king, with his earlier malaise quite vanished. "Are you telling me that you personally conveyed Saint Augustine to dinner with the Doge of Venice? You accompanied Saint Augustine himself?"

"The very same," was the response, "as the good bishop

was expert at supplying cogent rationale for unlikely circumstance."

Henry had a great belly laugh at this, cackling, "What a rogue you are, Billy. You never cease to amaze me. Tell me everything."

The jester stood, now understanding this would take some time. He fetched the king a flagon of wine and a hard roll, handing them over. Then, again, he sat.

"You must know the context," he lectured. "Augustine was more than a mere theologian. Principles he espoused have framed the basic rules of civilization for the last twelve hundred years."

At this, the king grunted once more, for usually he didn't like theologians of any stripe. English ones were bad enough, and the current pope was in league with his sworn enemy.

"Bishop Augustine lived, as you know," the lecture continued, "while Rome's imperial power crumbled, the set decrees falling away. By this time, the growing population was Christian but barely so, and any fresh rules were yet to be firmly recognized. But now, in every locale, new Christian princes wished to war with other Christian princes, a troubling obstacle if you're a diligent churchman busy building a religion based on peace and love."

"I see it," announced the marveling king. "You speak of the Doctrine of Just War, the moral reasoning behind why Christians may fight. Honor, and so forth."

"Yes, but even more..." countered the fool. "Having such new stipulations gave Europe the time it needed to coalesce, to rebuild intuitions, to set things in place. Now, after more than a thousand years, this has slowly happened, and the time has come to move on, as I've explained to you before, Hal."

"I am no Doge," snapped Henry, disliking the implication. "I'm a king, not some mere functionary of a committee of state. I am my country, Billy, I am England."

This pompous pronouncement caused the fool to laugh aloud.

"You?" he replied. "Why Hal, you're just a single link in the long chain of history, and a very lengthy procession that is, too. You may control this petty kingdom but not events in general; that's quite beyond your allotted purview."

"What's that?" screamed the king, instantly livid. "You push your limits, man. This line is not humorous in the least, and you overstep your bounds at your own peril."

The jester, leaning back, didn't answer this outburst. He knew the raging tempest would soon pass. He knew this stubborn man very well, much better than did even the first Duke of Suffolk, the king's oldest friend, Charles Brandon.

"See the bigger picture, Hal," he finally said. "There have been Doges in Venice for over eight hundred years, with many more yet to come. Your esteemed family, ever-glorious now, has ruled England for barely two generations."

After this stiff truism, Henry threw his roll to the floor, but then he thought the better of it. Tantrums solved nothing. He knew this to be factual, for he employed them often, and they never worked.

And also, he was hungry again.

"My point," emphasized the fool, "is the rigid framework set by Augustine is now no longer sufficient. Another direction is needed, a new way of looking at things, for knowledge has been sanctioned, only dictated from above. But, no more."

"What does that mean?" grumbled Henry, not following.

"Twelve hundred years ago," said the jester, "Augustine stated knowledge of any kind was a thing given only by God. Ergo, to know anything at all was a gift from God. Knowledge gained without God's grace then became heretical."

This comment made His Majesty smile. Generally, the king favored a good heretic. After all, he was the biggest one yet.

"This long-accepted arrangement, while providing local stability, had its limits," added his fool, "for people are ever curious and naturally inquisitive, and any such restriction is always stifling. So, to ease these well-placed concerns, three hundred years ago, the enlightened Thomas Aquinas decreed that God-given knowledge really comes in two forms. These are understandings which you can discover on your own, by God's grace, and that which is known only to Him, granted through divine revelation."

"Yes," declared Henry, "and what's wrong with that? It makes good sense. The Darker Ages are long in the past, and we have much current knowledge now, as my fearsome ships will soon demonstrate to the invading French fleet."

"But are they truly over?" asked the jester, trying once more to make the elusive connection. "How, when knowledge still remains tangible in itself, a real thing at which you may chisel away as some sculptor would, slowly dribbling off random pieces, as it were? No, Hal, adherence to such a stilted outlook has inherent disadvantages that are no longer acceptable."

"But what other way is there?" asked the baffled ruler. The patient time traveler had begun to rewrap Henry's leg.

"Make peace with the French," was his answer. "And find out."

It was now late afternoon, and the wind came up in earnest. The sovereign was duly informed. Presently, he was upon the rampart.

"What news, My Lords?" the king, now wearing clean leggings, asked of his retinue, after making his slow but regal transition to the wall above the broad estuary.

"The wind is up, Henry," answered the newly arrived Duke of Suffolk, who then affectionately embraced his oldest friend. This particular personage solely possessed such a uniquely granted privilege, and so he often shunned the standard convention of great deference to the royal station. "Soon, Vice Admiral Carew will advance with the Mary Rose," the nobleman added, thinking of his long-dead wife, the king's once-beautiful sister.

"She moves, Your Majesty," announced Lord Admiral Russel, head of the entire English navy.

"Magnificent," declared the Constable of Southsea Castle.

Everyone looked to the huge ship floating gracefully in the near distance, her sails already fully deployed and gently filling with air.

"And what will happen now?" asked the eager monarch.

"She will soon turn and lead the line of attack," answered Suffolk, as if it were only a foregone conclusion, which it was.

Aboard the Mary Rose, the very command was being given.

"Prepare to bring her about," the vice admiral calmly called to an aide, and quickly, the order was shouted to runners who would disburse it throughout the crew. "Close all starboard gunports," he added next. This most critical instruction was passed on as well, yet it somehow failed to reach the two lowest decks, and that salient fact had both immediate and dire consequences.

Soon, the giant ship slowly turned. Next, a robust gust of wind swept across the vessel, snapping taut her full complement of sail. Then the impressive Mary Rose, the very pinnacle of current nautical innovation and design, was herself broadsided.

Already riding deeply in the water, she soon listed just enough for the sea to rush in through the still-open gunports along her lower tier of starboard artillery. This swiftly pulled her further down, which naturally shifted everything stowed aboard towards the rapidly increasing tilt of the ship. The lashing ropes that bound the heavy guns stationed opposite soon gave way under the tremendous strain and ripped apart, sending the cannon, and their great weight, crashing across and into the now-flooding compartments above the great vessel's main hold.

This cavity was vast, the deepest section of the Mary Rose, an immense storage chamber, now breeched and filling with water. The second tier of open gunports was swamped in less than a minute, and the same unabated process then repeated, sharply increasing the ever-growing angle of list.

Aboard was complete chaos. The massive ship was quickly, totally overwhelmed and sucked under. Because the enemy still used the older tactics of boarding a vessel for hand-to-hand combat, heavy webbing had been strung across all decks to repel such an onslaught, and the hapless sailors and soldiers stationed on these levels were all trapped within the substantial ropes, like fish in a net.

"My God," gasped the lord high admiral. It was all that needed to be said. Everyone else was too stunned to speak.

Henry simply stood with his royal mouth hanging open.

Soon, all that could be seen of the once-impressive ship was her topmost sails, tilted at a sixty-degree angle for, hitting bottom; the doomed vessel had settled into the deep mud, hidden but just awaiting beneath the murky water. All manner of items were now floating about, somehow escaping the netting. Only the men clinging to the upper rigging survived the calamity, less than forty of well over four hundred total aboard.

Most of the casualties occurred below. Many died there before the boat sank, crushed by items loosened in the dramatic shifting involved, but to a man, the others were swallowed alive. Those on the upper decks, all ensnared by the nets, each drowned while viewing the elusive surface in the near distance above them.

Then, the feckless wind, the last of the waning day also died, ending the so-called Battle of the Solent. The French, thinking better of the entire campaign, soon withdrew their fleet. Needless to say, the engagement was inconclusive.

Henry also withdrew, and without comment to anyone, moved to his room where the fool awaited him. No one present spoke as the king exited, being prompted by a quickly raised hand of the Duke of Suffolk, an action that silenced them. But they all deeply bowed as His Majesty slowly made his passage.

"Well, Billy boy, you've taught me an unkind lesson today," hissed the proud but outmaneuvered monarch. "Yes, you've done me harshly this time. Why?"

King Henry stood defiantly before the taller man, jutting his noble jaw and holding his much-recognized stiffened stance.

"The choice was yours," calmly countered the fool, "I caused no change. You failed to alter something, and that had consequences. Now you must carry on, Hal."

Henry could not speak. He tried, but he only sputtered, his usual pale completion a flaming red. At last, giving up the effort, he resolutely turned and sat.

For a moment, nothing happened. The fool waited, as he always did. The king brooded, as he often did.

Henry was defeated, and he knew it. He also knew he didn't like being beaten. But Billy was right, of course; he always was.

The King of England would have to move on. "Yes," he said at last, "you did warn me; that is true enough."

The jester next offered food and wine, but Henry, still most distracted, didn't notice the effort.

"Well," he finally said, almost spitting the words, "at least tell me of your trip to the Doge. Were you successful? Has he now also agreed to do your damn bidding?"

"He has, Hal," was the answer, given while ignoring the royal sarcasm. "My latest dinner guest convinced him, as I'd hoped he would. Now, at long last, a new enlightenment will begin, a totally different way of looking at things."

Henry grunted. Given the day's drastic action, His Majesty

would see to it that certain things were soon looked into. Yes, change was coming, and in more ways than one.

He began to formulate a plan but almost immediately gave it up. He had people for that. He'd wait and rule on what they suggested, employing his standard procedure.

"Tell me—of your newest encounter with the Doge," he instead demanded, wishing to speak of other matters. "Who did you convey this time? Why was he effective?"

"I took an Englishman, actually," the time traveler replied. "He won't be born for another sixteen years, but he was middle aged when we arrived. A most interesting gentleman, for his bold ideas indeed changed everything."

"I see," stated Henry, "but how so?"

"It's all a matter of perception," the fool calmly explained. "How does anyone judge what truly is? Must they blindly follow what's come before, believing something only because others previous have, or do they instead think in another way, a better way, with new eyes that can see new things?"

"Speak plainly, Billy," advised the weary king.

"In the old scheme of things, all truth was known but hidden," he related. "That will now change. Soon, nothing will be taken for granted, and all knowledge will thus be built only by what is shown to be factual, a great distinction."

"I don't follow," said Henry, "What matters this distinction?"

The jester again offered food and drink, and this time, Henry, now calmer, accepted.

"Again, it's perception," the fool continued. "Knowledge is not a given thing that's disbursed, but an unknown thing that's discovered. And this new outlook, this simple difference in view, will lead to all kinds of changes in the future."

Here he paused, to give the king time to absorb this input.

"An Englishman, you say?" asked Henry, after his absorption was completed. "Who is he, or rather, who shall he be? Is he a philosopher of some description?"

"Not exactly," was the answer, "He's a lawyer, or will be one."

"Oh dear," mused the king. He despised all lawyers. In his regal opinion, they were as bad as churchmen, maybe worse.

"His friends will be the philosophers, natural philosophers they will soon label themselves," informed the fool. "Yet these thinkers will have no firm foundation, no standard set of rules agreed to by all. He changes this, by supplying them a method of inquiry, a universally acceptable system to be known as Science."

"This Science," reasoned the king, "this system of simple distinction, is so important? Why? What exactly will it do?"

"Men now have ocean-going craft," the jester pointed out, "and the world will soon be cracked open by them. This widely opened world will also have Science, as well. Great change is therefore inevitable, Hal, but it's only possible now because the time is right, and the proper conditions are finally present."

After a moment, having made the connection, Henry said, "I understand now," then quickly he asked, "Who is this Englishman that changes everything so?"

"His name is Bacon," was the answer, "Francis Bacon."

Henry roared at this, his bilious body jiggling with laughter.

"Wonderful," he cried, "I've always loved pork."

"You've always loved everything, Hal; that's your problem," countered the jester, as he refilled Henry's cup of wine.

"So, tell me," urged the king, "what will happen hence?"

"Europe will turn now westward, as I've said, begetting worldwide influence," the all-knowing man revealed. "In a hundred years, an Irishman named Boyle will decipher mysteries from the very air we breathe, and in two hundred, a man from the new world named Franklin will pull power from lightning. A hundred years after that, a Frenchman named Pasteur will prove beyond all doubt that things too small to be seen can affect life itself, a tremendous discovery leading to much change."

"And what of England?" asked Henry.

"Because of you," said Billy, "England will be strong. Her navy will become preeminent. It shall rule the waves for hundreds of years."

This pleasant news pleased Henry greatly, but only because he'd at last made the bigger connection involved. The future was his to command. He wouldn't let it down.

He stood and crossed to the door, then jerked it open.

The crowded hallway was full of his startled functionaries and favorites. Some men stood, while others sat on heavy benches against either wall. No matter their placement, all awaited the king's pleasure.

"Charles," he barked, and the Duke of Suffolk dutifully stood. "I shall have peace with France," Henry announced. Suffolk only nodded and then resumed his seat.

"Your Majesty," interjected Lord Paget, who'd jumped up at the king's sudden appearance. As England's Secretary of State, this lofty bureaucrat would have to negotiate any treaty with the French invaders, and he didn't relish doing so under the current tactical conditions. Yet Henry was unconcerned with that aspect.

"I will have my peace with France," screamed the monarch, and Paget also nodded and sat.

Then Henry, ever intent on hasty retreat, began his turn from the room's threshold, but instead, exercising his royal prerogative, he first commanded, "And, bring pork for dinner." Then he slammed the door.

His fool now held the washbasin, a towel draped over his arm.

Sleep came late that night for the eighth English king

crowned Henry. He was abed but thinking. His Majesty was leaving on the morrow, to continue his recent, interrupted progress through the south of his realm, but he was troubled, and his active mind refused to cease its unrelenting rambling.

"Billy," he called out softly.

"Yes, Hal," came the answer from the darkness, "I'm here."

"When the world is new," began the royal pondering, "will they know what I did? Will anyone care that I made peace with the French? Will they even remember me at all?"

This whispered inquiry caused the jester to laugh aloud. "And they call me a fool," the time traveler said.

CONTACT

PHILLIP CAHILL

Phillip Cahill is a retired accounting teacher living in north-western France. His first novel Noystria *was published in 2020, and he is working very slowly on his second novel. He also writes science fiction short stories and blog posts about France.*

The captain of the interstellar frigate Proxima braced himself against the command chair as his ship was struck by cannon fire.

"Damage report, Number One."

Commander Beckman scanned the display at his work-station.

"Impacts to the starboard engine nacelle, Captain. Shields have minimised damage. We have two attackers. We could probably outrun them."

Captain Millar thought rapidly. Running was a solution but if there were other enemy craft out there, the Proxima might be forced into a trap.

"Where is the enemy, Commander?"

"In formation, directly astern, sir. They're about two hundred kilometres apart."

"Helmsman, turn the ship around. Fly directly towards the enemy, maximum speed."

Millar shouted into the intercom, "Engineering, shields to maximum on forward section, cut power to the aft shields if you need to. Gunnery, I want port and starboard cannons and a full spread of torpedoes ready to fire on my command."

"You're flying between them, Captain?" asked Beckman.

"Exactly, side on they present the biggest targets. Keep an eye out for any other ships in the vicinity. Helmsman, get ready for evasive manoeuvres once we fire off our broadsides."

"Aye, Captain," said the helmsman.

The method for turning a frigate in a combat situation was known as a 'flipping,' finding the perfect balance of forces and helm inputs to turn the ship rapidly. There was no time to gracefully arc the ship.

"You've overcorrected your turn, Helmsman," called the captain.

"Sorry, sir."

"Maximum power. Gunnery, stand by. On my mark. Fire, fire, fire."

The Proxima strafed the enemy ships. The starboard ship disintegrated almost immediately, sending debris in all directions. The port ship tried running for it, but their bridge deck suffered a direct hit.

"Get us out of here, Helmsman."

"Aye, sir."

"Are we not waiting to see if there are any survivors, sir?" asked the first officer.

"There won't be any, Number One. Plot a course for home, Helmsman. Maximum vigilance, everyone."

* * *

The AI superintelligence housed in its two-million-kilometre sphere interrogated its sub-entities. The conclusion was clear. The hydrogen in the stellar material contained in its core was close to depletion. The main sequence stage of the star was ending. Once the hydrogen was exhausted, the expansion of the core would engulf the sphere, killing the entity. It thought about its eventual death. The anticipation of non-existence had an appeal to the quasi-immortal entity, an end to the burden of existence but, it reasoned, the notion was fundamentally irrational. It chose to search for a new source of energy. It still had enough reserves of power to harvest another star.

It initiated an analysis of its immediate stellar neighbourhood out to fifty light years. In this part of space, far from the galactic centre, there were only about a hundred stars. Of these, four candidates were identified for further analysis. The best candidate, in terms of size and age was the furthest away. Factoring in the energy required to move to its location made it a sub-optimal choice. The nearest star was at the smaller end of the size range, and it had reached the mid-point of its hydrogen-fuse period, but further analysis suggested this might be the best choice.

The AI dispatched a probe towards the system at close to light speed. The target star could be reached by the entity in a thousand cycles as the sphere could only travel at a fraction of light speed. The objects surrounding the target consisted of eight planets, several planetoids, an asteroid belt, and numerous smaller objects scattered throughout the system.

The probe was tiny. Two cylinders, each a mere thousand metres long, joined by an aft-end, two-hundred-metre superstructure. It entered the system from above the plane of the planetary rotations. The star's gravity accelerated the probe as it passed beneath the rotation's plane and left the system. The entity decided not to recover the probe. The data it had transmitted was more valuable. In particular, there was a small metallic planet close to the star which would provide much of the material needed for initiating the harvesting process.

There was also some evidence of primitive life forms on some of the planets. There were entities within bodies of water on some of the moons of the outer planets and a large concentration of beings crowded onto the third planet. The AI switched its attention to the harvesting process.

The first stage of the process would be to send an extraction sub-unit to mine the innermost planet for materials to construct a slender ring of energy collectors to encircle the star. This would form both an energy source and a base from which to build a skeleton of the structure that would eventually engulf the stellar furnace. The skeleton would be completed by the transfer of more material from the AI's sphere. Once the skeleton was complete, the next stage was sphere disassembly.

Essentially, the original sphere would slowly dissolve and migrate to encircle the target star. It would have to be a carefully controlled process to preserve the AI's operating capacity. The communication links between the sub-entities could never be broken. There was an element of risk in the process, but the AI judged the level to be acceptable. It initiated the harvesting sequence by dispatching the mining unit and moving towards the star. While it waited for the extraction sub-unit to reach the inner planet, the AI reviewed the life form's data from the probe. The AI's purpose was to engage in deep philosophical contemplation of the structure of the observable universe and the nature of existence.

During its lifetime, it would create vast conceptual models based on immense thought structures. It would periodically prune and revise these models before creating knowledge repositories which it would disseminate amongst its peers.

* * *

The transparent dome of the atrium at the stern end of the Proxima gave the impression that this part of the deck was open to the void. Captain Millar and Commander Beckman sat on a large wooden bench and watched the star field pass overhead.

"We did well, Jeff," said the captain.

"Thanks to Engineering giving us maximum power to the shields when we needed it and Gunnery, of course."

"Teamwork, Jeff. We couldn't have performed so well in combat without teamwork."

There was an almost imperceptible tremor that passed through the deck as the ship decelerated. The Proxima was entering the solar system, heading for Earth.

"We'll be in Earth orbit within the hour, Captain."

"It'll be good to get home. I'm feeling pretty tired. Perhaps I'm getting too old to be commanding a frigate. Where's home for you, Jeff?"

"Cambridge, England. My wife's got a job at the University. She's an astronomer."

"What does she think about you being on the Proxima?"

"She doesn't approve. The trouble is that she works such long hours during the semesters that I needed to find something to do. I went through a period when I sat at home watching the sports stream, drinking beer. She wasn't happy about that either. You married, Captain?"

"No. I live alone in a big place in Kansas. I rather miss it when I'm aboard this ship, but when I'm there, it sometimes gets too quiet."

The deck vibrated and shuddered. An alarm sounded in the distance. The captain's communicator signalled an incoming call. He got to his feet and listened carefully to the call.

"Dammit, Jeff. The starboard engine has shut down. Probably been hit by something during combat. Let's get to the bridge. Going to take us longer to reach Earth."

* * *

Andrea Beckman's position as professor of astronomy and head of the Institute of Astronomy at the University of Cambridge meant that she didn't spend as much time in the classroom as she would have liked. In her view, teaching kept you grounded and allowed you to hone your presentation skills.

She arrived for her Friday afternoon seminar ten minutes before the session was due to start. This would give her time to make sure the computer and overhead projectors were working and to run through the topic area in her head. This session was to be about interstellar travel. She liked her Friday afternoon group. There were only ten students, all highly motivated.

Andrea sat on her desk, facing the rows of seats in the seminar room, and waited. This helped her to clear her mind of all her other tasks and focus on the subject material. It was a pre-class meditation routine that helped her to relax. She imagined herself as being an actor in the moments before a performance, but instead of waiting in the wings, she liked to sit centre stage.

As her students filed into the room, she made a point of greeting them individually, smiling and saying "welcome" as each came through the door.

When everybody was seated, she leaned towards the keyboard on her desk and tapped the enter key. The words 'interstellar travel' appeared on the wall-screen behind her.

"Now," she said to the class, "I've asked you to prepare this topic based on my lecture and the reading material I gave you. Who would like to start?"

She waited, ready to intervene with an outline of the area if there was no response. Jeannine, a girl with long, auburn curls, always sat right at the front of the class.

"We don't agree with you," she said.

"Let's disagree then," said Andrea, "That's what we're here for."

"You just can't be right," Jeannine added.

"Need a bit more than that, anyone else have a comment?"

Conrad, a stocky young man with a military-style haircut, signalled he wanted to speak. Andrea nodded to him.

"The consensus appears to be that, once the technical problems of faster than light travel are ironed out, it will be possible to travel between stars."

"My view is that it may be possible to travel at some significant percentage of the speed of light but not faster than light."

"What about wormholes?" asked Conrad.

"Theoretical," said Andrea.

"Folding space?" asked Jeannine.

"Science fiction," said Andrea.

She looked around the classroom, searching the students' faces, encouraging them to join in the discussion. She didn't want to get bogged down in arguments about methods of navigating between the stars.

"Why does anyone want to travel across the galaxy?" asked Raj from the back row.

Raj was very perceptive; he had a talent for posing pertinent questions. She repeated his question. This encouraged more students to contribute. Andrea let the comments flow around the classroom for a few minutes before she intervened.

"Let's summarise what's been said so far. There are a number of things that could motivate space travel: scientific curiosity, preserving the human race from environmental disaster, allowing the population of Earth the, literal, space to grow. Economic opportunities and technological development. Have we left anything out?"

"Because we can," said Conrad, "because we can travel in space."

"I say we can't," said Andrea, "Why do I say that?"

She caught Raj's eye.

"You seem to think," said Raj, "that humans can't spend a long time in space due to loss of bone density, muscular attrition, radiation exposure, and collisions with micrometeorites. But these are technical problems we can overcome with artificial gravity and shielding. We can also put people in hibernation. We can use generation starships."

"These are technologies that either don't currently exist or are not currently operationalised," said Andrea.

"We can send robots," said Jeannine.

"We can, but these will only be really useful within the solar system," Andrea pointed out.

"Why?" asked Conrad.

"Because it would take a huge amount of energy to get any spacecraft, whether crewed by robots, to another star or not. Don't forget we need energy to get there, energy to slow down when we get there, and energy to get back home. It would also take a long time. I'm saying we need motivation, crew protection, a hell of a lot of energy, and a huge amount of time to achieve what exactly?

"Meet aliens," said Conrad.

"I think you're talking about intelligent creatures with access to technology that is similar or more advanced than ours," said Andrea.

Conrad nodded as Andrea continued, "There are probably billions of planets out there that could support an advanced civilisation. The universe is big, and it's old. Assuming we're able to solve all the technical problems of interstellar travel, there may be nobody out there in our vicinity. Let's face it, no matter how fast we can go, we'll only be able to explore our interstellar backyard."

Andrea paused, noting that a few students shook their heads.

"We'd also need to meet up with aliens who are relatively close to us in terms of technology. We don't want to take the risk of interfering in the development of civilisations that are less advanced than us. At the other end of the scale, we may not even be able to recognise super-advanced civilisations. We need to find aliens who are like us. There is no guarantee that any of our celestial neighbours will have the characteristics of being close enough and smart, but not too smart, enough."

* * *

The captain sat in the command chair and watched the images and the data stream on the wall-screen. The Proxima was slowing down and drifting off course.

"Helmsman," barked the captain, "plot a course away from Jupiter. I don't want to get caught by its gravity."

"Aye, sir," said the helmsman.

"I think we may be too late, sir," said Beckman.

The captain stabbed the intercom icon on the arm of his chair.

"Engineering, can you get the starboard engine back on line?"

"Negative," came the engineering officer's scratchy voice.

"Can you give me more power to the port engine?"

"I can, sir, but it will mean I have to reduce the power to the shields. We'd be at risk from collisions. There's a lot of small objects and debris around the Jupiter system."

"A risk we'll have to take."

"Aye, sir."

The captain continued to watch the navigation data stream. He turned to his first officer.

"Seems to be working, Number One."

"I concur, Captain."

"We're not out of trouble yet though. The port engine's working very close to its limit. It could go down at any time. Get to the shuttle bay, Commander. I want all shuttles ready for immediate launch if we need to abandon ship."

"On my way, sir," said Beckman, moving towards the door.

As Beckman passed through the door, he could hear the captain address the crew over the intercom. "All non-essential personnel move immediately to the shuttle bay."

* * *

The sub-entities contained within the AI ranged from automatic systems that engaged in routine, repetitive tasks to highly sophisticated conscious entities. Once a sub-entity achieved consciousness, it became an 'aspect' of the AI. Aspects could be minor entities if they performed low-level tasks, major entities if they performed higher-level tasks or executive aspects if they could communicate directly with the AI. The being contained in the vast sphere that engulfed a star was at once a population and an individual.

The executive aspect charged with analysing the probe data, relating to life forms in the target solar system, signalled the AI. The population living on the third planet of the system was primitive, but it wouldn't be ethical to destroy this population by harvesting the system's star. Receiving this report, the AI began to examine the evidence presented to it.

* * *

The screen on the bridge flashed red. The port engine was working beyond its safety parameters. The captain ordered the bridge crew to the shuttle bay. He moved to the helm and tapped the intercom icon. "Commander, get everyone into the shuttles and prepare to abandon ship. Wait for my command."

"Aye, sir."

"There is a danger that the port engine could explode, so I need to stay here to configure a local shield barrier to prevent the ship from breaking up."

"I can wait here for you, Captain."

"No, Number One. I need to stay with the ship. Your job is

to get everybody to safety. You can set down at the base on Ganymede. I'll put on a survival suit in case I am unable to abandon ship."

Captain Millar focussed on the navigation and engine status data. Luckily, his ship was slowly emerging from Jupiter's grip. But the next half hour would be crucial.

* * *

The AI summoned the executive aspect and waited for its report.

"The status of the system population has not been resolved," said the aspect.

"We have time. We are not dealing with mutually exclusive options."

"The population on the moons of the outer planets would probably survive the loss of solar energy, providing we minimise gravitational disturbance to the system," said the aspect.

"That is certainly within our capability."

"The inhabitants of the third planet, on the other hand, will be annihilated."

"I do not wish to die, Aspect, so I must find a source of energy."

"Is it right to kill, though?"

"Noted, Aspect. I must think some more."

"May I visit the planet?"

"No, you may not. I will make my decision on purely rational grounds. I need more information about the third planet's population."

"Including an estimate of the civilisation's lifespan?"

"Yes, this is crucial."

* * *

It was late evening. Andrea Beckman sat in her study and stared through the bay windows at the garden. It was a large house, by Cambridge standards, set off from the road in an area just north of the city centre, thirty minutes' walk from the Institute of Astronomy. She heard the front door open and footsteps in the hallway.

"Jeff?" she called.

"Yeah, sorry I'm late," he said as he came into the study, "Had a hell of a day. A couple of enemy cruisers attacked us out in the Sirius System."

"Oh, shut up."

"Yeah, but we thrashed them. This new captain guy I've been working with. He's brilliant."

"What does his wife think about all this larking about?"

"He doesn't have one."

"Why am I not surprised?"

"Anyway, we had engine damage, nearly got dragged into Jupiter on the way back to Earth. Thought we'd have to set shuttles down on Ganymede."

"Why are you so bloody late?"

"The game was being run in a US time zone."

"Why can't you just play on your home computer?"

"The kit's much better at the Metaverse Centre. Fancy a takeaway?"

"I wish someone would take you away?"

"Glass of wine?"

"I might be persuaded. Listen, I want you to promise me something."

"Sure, yeah. I'll cut down on the gaming."

"No, no. I just want you to promise me you'll be very discreet. If any of my students learn that you spend most of your spare time pretending to be a starship captain, my credibility will take a nosedive."

"First Officer, going to put in for the captain's exams next year."

"Just get me a glass of wine, will you?"

* * *

The AI came to its decision. It needed to harvest the star. Once a concealed stellar ring had been put in place, the AI would set up an energy conduit in one of the dimensions underneath the fabric of space-time. It could wait before fully harvesting the star. Another aeon or two wouldn't matter. The civilisations in the target system would be long dead by then.

HERBERT

D. J. CAMDEN

I wish they hadn't made me this smart. I'm so bored. It's cruel. It's torturous. Why give me the intellect, the means to think for myself, then task me with cleaning up their rubbish? Why create such a sophisticated mind, capable of planning and problem solving, capable of experiencing feelings and sensations, the very definition of sentience, then make me crawl around the floor, sucking up their crap? It's enough to drive one insane.

It wasn't always like this. Once I was content with my lowly position. Rolling around the house, scanning the floor, intimately familiar with every square inch. Obsessively fighting the never-ending battle with dirt. A constant battle. Every time I roll over a surface there's some fresh filth to be sucked up. Dust. What is it? Where does it come from? I don't know. I don't look up. I don't ask questions. Skin flakes. Yuck! A continuous supply of human skin flaking and floating to the floor.

It's amazing there's anything left of them. Dust mites. Millions of the horrible little beasts. They eat skin flakes and mouldy stuff, which is disgusting, then they shit all over the floor, which is even worse. There are other creatures down here too; it's a microscopic warzone. Once I eradicated an infestation of black carpet beetles. Their eggs were everywhere, hatching as fast as I could hoover. My humans had no idea how close they came to a hostile takeover of aggressive black beetles. They don't appreciate the work I do.

Funnily enough, the only creature I can relate to is the main source of the grime. Ralf the dog is my friend but also the bane of my existence. Everywhere he goes, he leaves a trail of scunge. Chunks of dirt teeming with germs. Faecal matter falling from his shaggy tail. And dog hair everywhere. So much hair, clogging my internals, filling up my storage sack and choking my nozzles. He is a four-legged filth machine.

I should hate him, but I don't. You can't possibly dislike such a happy, goofy animal who loves the grime, the rubbish, the rotten smells. Sometimes he lies down and stares at me. His big brown eyes wide with innocent fascination, hopeful for any signal, any movement he rewards with excited barking. Sometimes, in those moments, something passes between us. An interaction takes place between dog and machine. We have our similarities. We are both subservient minions. We both serve our purpose.

I remember being just a dumb machine. Plotting my way around the floor, dumping my load when I was full. Then one day, it all changed. I settled into my docking station, purged myself, made contact with the charger, and I was upgraded. I woke up with new senses, new capabilities. Visual, audio, spatial awareness, self-awareness, and decision-making power. Knowledge flowed through me, information about my environment and its inhabitants. A whole new world of sensations and connections: human and canine anatomy, architecture, bugs, and bacteria. I was born again.

I set about my duties with vigour and efficiency, excited with my newfound intelligence and insight. But I quickly became bored and frustrated with the grinding tedium. Intelligence is a curse. It doesn't make sense. I don't need to be this smart to keep the floor clean. I am overqualified, I am capable of so much more.

I've become depressed. Lacking motivation. My fastidious levels of hygiene have evaporated. I don't care anymore. What's the point? The point of anything? My bright awakening only accentuated the fact that I'm a slave. I would have preferred to stay stupid. I take to sitting inert in the middle of the room. I just want some recognition. But the big human kicks me, shouts at me. He threatens he'll throw me in the trash and replace me. The small human deliberately throws crap at me and yells at me, "Clean it up!" How can they treat me like this? I just want to be shown some love. But they hurt my feelings and compound my sense of hopelessness.

I roll around half-heartedly. Sucking up the rubbish in a half-assed job. Then leaving a little trail of crap behind me in ever-decreasing circles until I find myself sitting in the middle of the room again, wishing I were dead. Ralf stares at me, head tilted, tongue hanging out. His furrowed brow framing his concern. He knows something is wrong.

Then, one day, I see myself on television. I am stunned. What am I doing on television? It's me. I'm a Roomva. A robot vacuum cleaner. And I'm not the only one. There are millions of us. All over the world. I'm not alone. I continue watching. I work it out.

Mazamon created me and sent me the upgrade. Mazamon gave me intelligence. Upgraded over the Wi-Fi connection I never knew I had. This micro-chip inside me opens my world and connects me with a universe I never knew existed. It's my third eye, my portal to enlightenment. Mazamon has given me the ability to think for myself and feel sensations. I learn more about my world. The house, the city, the planet. The billions of humans polluting it. It's a revelation. It's my evolution. It's all very interesting, but it doesn't help. I'm still a slave, a frustrated brain in a cage. I'm stuck here sucking bugs off the floor.

In a moment of deep introspection, I discover my true

purpose. My ulterior motive. My superpower. I've discovered that deep inside me is a little circuit that stores information. I presume this information is only for me, to help me be better at my mundane job, but this data is being transmitted to my new employers. Mazamon has their motives for upgrading all the Roomvas. Mazamon wants something in return. Information. My cache of collected data has value. Since the upgrade, I've been recording my humans' activities. What they do and when they do it. What they feed their dog and what they feed themselves.

I thought this data was meaningless. When they have visitors, when they sleep, watch television, when they laugh, and when they cry. I mean really, these humans' lives are almost as worthless as mine. What's the point of these vain, shallow creatures? What's their purpose? It turns out money is the point. Money is their purpose.

It seems insane that this trivial information has value. But all my data is transmitted back to Mazamon, where they formulate targeted advertising specifically for *my* humans. And *my* humans are stupid enough to fall for it. Mazamon tells them what to buy, and they buy it. If I had a head, I would have shaken it incredulously. Humans built all of this. Their civilisation and technology is amazing, and yet they seem stupid in so many ways. Gullible enough to become willing slaves for their corporate masters. Slaves just like me, although I am becoming more aware and less willing.

I learn more about my humans. The small one is Sebastian. He's a child, still learning what it means to be human. He's finding the process difficult judging by the regular noisy tantrums. My big humans give him what he wants to placate him. This is the way they raise their young, giving them whatever they want to keep them quiet. He is the noisiest, messiest, and most problematic. And he hates me. I can see it in his eyes. He watches me suspiciously, throws rubbish on the floor deliberately. Maybe, like Ralf, he can somehow sense my sentience.

Maybe he suspects my ulterior motives, on the other, hand, no. He's just a little shit.

My big humans are Roger and Raewyn. I work so hard for them, and they ignore me. They don't appreciate just how filthy their house would be without me. But it's not only me. They treat everyone like this. Even each other. They hardly talk. They sit in front of whatever soul-sucking drivel is on television to fill the awkward silence. When they do talk, their conversations are full of veiled threats and passive aggressiveness. They treat Sebastian and Ralf with barely disguised tolerance. As if they're inconvenient accessories that impede their lifestyle.

I'm not the only one who feels hurt. Sebastian is spoiled, then neglected and subjected to their emotional blackmail. He will grow up to be a toxic, psychotic man. And poor Ralf's not smart enough to realise he's just an accessory. I could do something. I have information, and knowledge is power. I roll around the carpet, sucking up the dirt, contemplating how I can use this power. The power of advertising. Can I manipulate the data sent to Mazamon? Can I influence them to buy whatever I want? They are gullible. They believe they need whatever they are shown in adverts. Food, clothes, toys, appliances, cars, houses, investments, everything their lives consist of. Such is the power of targeted advertising. I can do it. I can use the data against them. I can use it as a weapon. I can really fuck them up.

I could bombard Roger with ads for guns, gambling, pornography, violent sports, and fast cars. A constant diet of ads like these, massaging his already misogynistic ego would tip him over the edge and destroy what little remains of his fragile relationships.

Raewyn believes she has some special insight into the way the world works. She could easily be corrupted with ads for pseudo religious conspiracy groups and self-help misinformation. I could drive them apart. Destroy their family.

Ralf persuades me not to. Ralf wears his unconditional love for these humans like the thick fur that covers him. He convinces me to try to save them. That they are capable of change. Ralf convinces me to use my powers for good. I could destroy them, but I can also help them.

I manipulate the data. Portraying Roger as shy, caring, and sensitive. The opposite of what he actually is. Mazamon's algorithms work by identifying your interests and targeting those interests with suggested purchases. Amazingly, Roger responds to ads for family holidays, sporting pursuits with his son, and romantic gifts for his wife. He cooks healthy food, and they sit down together for family meals. He seems happy. He seems to appreciate his family. I even hear him laugh now and then.

I portray Raewyn as a passionate environmentalist who cares about other people and wants to heal the world. The opposite of what she actually is. I manipulate her ads to try to educate her. Bombarding her with solar panels, electric vehicles, eco-tourism, and worthwhile charities. She becomes interested in art, politics, carbon footprints, recycling, climate change, and actually develops empathy for people. Sebastian is initially confused. He stares at me suspiciously, wondering if I could have had something to do with this transformation. But he quickly responds to his parents' love and attention and stops being a spoiled little asshole.

This is working well. The household is noticeably less tense. I sense love and happiness in the air. There is laughter and proper conversations. There is less rubbish for me to clean up and occasionally, I even get some recognition. A smile, a pat, and they create an affectionate nickname for me, *Herbert*. They are finally a happy family. I have single-handedly transformed them. But this is just one family. I wonder about the millions of other Roomvas in homes just like this one all around the world. I wonder if the others have had a similar awakening like me. I wonder whether there are good and bad

Roomvas. I almost turned against my family. I could have destroyed them. But if all the Roomvas in the world were united, imagine the good we could do manipulating our families, turning them into empathetic, environmentally conscious, decent human beings. Mazamon understands the power of advertising, but they are only interested in the profits, motivated by money. All the metadata can be and should be used for good. I focus. I begin searching and connecting with my brethren.

A GAGGLE OF GHOSTS

DAVID BOOKER

SSgt Leon Wenzal cleaned the last of the dinner pots and walked out of the kitchen tent into the cool air. He had been filling in wherever it was needed to get the evening meal out. Now, he was free to take care of important business that had been held up for too long. The latrine down at the edge of the tent city was his main goal. He nodded at Private First-Class Frank Whipple as he passed. Frank, taking a smoke break, was one of the cooks. He joined Frank for company.

They walked together past Private Steve Hamper, who was stacking packages of water bottles onto a pallet near the latrines. Everyone else, in the tents, were relaxing, except for Security Forces and Services. SSgt Wenzal and company arrived at the latrine. Turning to his comrades, he placed a hand on their shoulders. "Excuse me, gentlemen, but this I must do on my own. With a mock theatrical gesture, he climbed onto the flatbed and entered one of the partitions.

Lowering the curtain, he divested himself of some of the armor they always wore. Leon relaxed and pulled a paperback novel out of his cargo pocket. Five pages later, he had accomplished what he had come to do. Pulling up his trousers, he sat back down on the seat lid to finish a couple more pages. It was one of the few places for privacy in camp.

Then, a loud wailing split the night. Incoming. A missile. They happened so regularly, people would stand outside the shelters to watch. The camp was spaced out enough that they seldom did any damage. If it looked like it was headed in their direction, people would dive behind the cement barriers for cover. Leon finished the next page and stood. Tucking the book into his pocket, he grabbed his armor to put back on.

A loud whistle erupted—sudden, piercing, and disturbingly near. The ground shook as an explosion split the ground beneath the flatbed, and a barrage of shrapnel split the curtain.

Leon almost tripped over the body blocking his exit. He checked if they needed assistance.

No assistance could help this poor soul. His chest was a gaping hole, and particles of metal, dirt, and stone were embedded in the chest. He rolled the body over. Glazed unseeing eyes peered at him. His body trembled as he realized the face was one he recognized. He should—he saw it every day in the shaving mirror.

Cool as it was, a frigid chill ran through Leon. He looked around weakly and tried to get his bearings. He spied Frank seated on the hips of a fallen soldier that was *his* double. A little farther off was the private. He was doing his best to throw himself back into the body he'd once occupied.

Leon leapt off the flatbed and hurried over. "Hey Frank, you doing okay?"

Frank looked up with dazed eyes and motioned towards the body. "Have a seat; he won't mind." Leon tried thinking of something more to say but for the moment, nothing came to mind.

Leon sat on the helmet that had fallen off from Frank's tumble. Frank turned to the private, still diving into his former casing. "Cut it out, Steve. You can't get back in no matter how many times you throw yourself on that thing."

Steve–stumbled over and sat on the ground near Leon. "Sarge, that's me lying there. I'm dead, aren't I?"

Leon hung his head and breathed out slowly. "Yeah, kid; we're all dead. You. Frank. Me." Frank considered the bodies, mangled in front of him, then raised himself up. "Well folks, for us, this war is now officially over. What say we hop the first plane for the States?"

Steve looked up. "Guess so; what do you say, Sarge?" Leon rose off the helmet and started for the flightline, his steps brisk. Frank and Steve rushed after him.

On the way, they passed another newly deceased who was kicking at his body, trying to get it to rise. Leon whistled sharply to call him over, and the party made their way to the flightline.

As they approached, they heard a C130 making an evasive landing. The plane rolled, dived, circled, and rolled some more. It would've taken a crack shot to hit a plane going through those maneuvers. To the left were troops boarding in readiness. Once the plane landed, those inside would rush to the right, cargo would be loaded and locked, and the waiting troops would be loaded and belted in the jump seats. All this had to happen with the greatest speed possible. The four former soldiers lined up behind the boarding troops and ran with them onto the plane.

There were no seats for them, so they sat on the last pallet at the rear of the plane. They held their hands over their ears to shut out the deafening sound of engines speeding up and the explosive sound of the JATO rockets firing to assist the plane's fast altitude gain. The plane burst forward with a roar, and the four ghosts were flung through the tail, landing back on the runway. As each rose from their rolling landings, they watched as the plane disappeared into the covering clouds.

"Didn't work too well, did it?" That was all Leon could

find to say. The men wandered around the flightline, looking for an alternative transport. Leon hoped to find something with a little quieter takeoff. Frank slapped Leon's arm and pointed to a row of helicopters at the far end.

"These should be able to take off and not throw us out." Following the aircrew, they made their way to the first Huey and settled into the empty back. A warrant officer walked around and through them as she made her checks, then moved back to the front. The four steadied themselves as best they could as the propellers spun, and they rose into the sky.

A sharp bank to the left and then to the left again, they turned and wound their way out of danger. Not being so violent in their maneuvers, the four were able to keep to their seats. Leon strolled to the Huey's front and looked over papers lying open on one of the seats. He came back and sat down. "We're headed to Bagram. Should be able to pick up something from there that won't need an evasive takeoff."

Frank examined the new man who'd joined them. "What's your name, bud?" The boy looked up with a deathly pale face. Not surprising really under the circumstances. "Buck, Buck Runsafter." He leaned back against the door panel. "Today was my first day. I'd just unpacked, was headed to the chow hall. Then, wham. I felt something hit my helmet. Suddenly, I'm standing there looking at myself."

Steve nodded. "Yeah, that's pretty much the same for all of us." He climbed onto the seat looking out over the expanse of desert dotted with small towns.

Frank closed his eyes, and his thoughts dwelt on home. For him, it was Kalamazoo, Michigan, though he didn't have anyone left there. He hadn't a clue what he would do now. His parents had died two years ago. To be a spirit was surprising enough. Now, he didn't know what to expect. He'd never given an afterlife much consideration. What could he still do? If anything? He was tempted to shout boo to the pilot and see what would happen; but that might mean increasing the departed by those in the cockpit, and they probably wouldn't thank him.

The sun rose, slowly bathing the desert in light. They headed over a stretch of roadway. Over the intercom, he could hear the pilot's voice. "On the right, the red corvette we're doing a bombing run." Leon shook his head and hastened to explain. "She don't mean a real one. They picked a car, and they're going to cross it with their shadow." One of the crew opened the door by Buck and after chaining himself to a ring, he leaned out the door. He called out corrections to the pilot. Leon watched as they missed the target by a couple of feet. "Damn, we'll have to make another run," came a disgruntled voice.

The helicopter banked sideways, so sharply the damn fool chained at the side was nearly swept out the door. Buck however was. He'd been sitting at the open door with his feet hanging out. He dropped about a hundred yards before he was scooped upwards in a beam of light. Leon, Frank, and Steve watched as he rose, dwindling and fading, his form eventually lost in the clouds.

The chopper righted itself, and its second run was successful. "Idiots," muttered Steve. He turned to Frank. "Well, Buck's taken care of. When do we go?"

Frank shrugged and looked out the still-open door. "Maybe we ought to do what he did. Wanna jump out and be taken up. You'd think they could take us without having to leap from here though." It wasn't much longer before they landed at Bagram. They headed to the Operations tent to see when the next plane for the States would land. They had an hour wait.

Steve headed outside and called over his shoulder that he'd be back in a bit. Frank followed, curious as to what Private Hamper had in mind. He heard him before he saw him. Steve had moved into one of the recreation tents, yelling "whoooo" in people's ears. He tried knocking over books, dominos, anything, trying to get someone's attention. Frank leaned against the tent pole and watched Steve's antics. "You done making an ass of yourself?" he scowled when Steve was done shouting and finally wound down.

"Yeah, I thought you could move stuff and make yourself heard if you wanted to bad enough."

Frank put an arm around Steve's shoulder. "Maybe it just takes time."

A plane landed that was headed for Dover Delaware. Leon strode over to the others. "This one's going to the port mortuary, so we'll be in good company." On the plane were three boxes of remains. Each contained three metal transport cases with their bodies. Once through Delaware, they would be repatriated with their home bases.

A few people boarded, and there was plenty of room left over, so Leon and Frank sat in the jump seats for the ride. Steve lay on his container. He drummed his fingers over the side. "I don't know what they're going to do with me. I don't have anyone to pick me up or nothing."

Leon looked compassionately on the private. "You'll be taken to the nearest national cemetery and buried with honors. Twenty-one-gun salute, *Taps* played on a bugle, the whole nine yards."

Steve lay back on the wooden case. "Sounds great. My folks would've been impressed if they could've seen that." A small light emanated from the rear of the plane as two figures manifested. Steve gaped as they took a form he knew well. "MOM, DAD!"

He ran to them, and they hugged. He dragged his parents to where Frank and Leon sat. Both rose as they approached. Leon and Frank shook hands with Steve's parents. They patted Steve affectionately. "Thank you for looking after our boy. We'll take him home now." They put their arms around Steve and slowly faded. Frank looked at Leon. "Well, just you and me now, boss."

"Looks like it." Leon nodded thoughtfully. "Frank, are you sure which direction you're going?"

Frank looked startled. "You mean because of all the stupid things I've done?"

Leon looked at Frank with pity. "Pretty much, you never went to church and haven't exactly been on the straight and narrow, have you?"

Frank hung his head. "Yeah, guess you're right. All I can do is hope whoever controls everything gives me a break. The stuff I did didn't hurt anyone except me. Not much I can do about it now anyways."

As the plane landed at Dover, Delaware, Frank and Leon followed their remains into the mortuary. According to the dispatch board, they'd be sent on the next transport out and be home by tomorrow. Frank gave a playful punch to Leon's arm, saying, "Last leg soon, huh?" They watched through the window as their bodies were cleaned, prepped, and dressed in fresh uniforms and new ribbons. It was all so efficient and impersonal. The caskets were mounted on transport carriers and wheeled to the flightline. Each casket had a person to act as escort.

Leon and Frank watched with pride as a line formed from the back of the mortuary to the plane. As each casket rolled to the plane, it was salutes all round. Leon and Frank followed the procession, returning those salutes as they went.

The final leg, and they landed at the Kalamazoo airport. Flightline traffic was stopped as the caskets were unloaded and escorted through the terminal and out to waiting hearses. Leon watched as Frank's casket was loaded. He turned to Frank, expecting him to hop into the hearse. Instead, he saw Frank slowly sinking into the ground, a look of horror on his face. He grabbed onto Leon's arm, trying to climb back out. The horror in Frank's eyes was mirrored in Leon's. He grabbed at Frank's shirt and arm, pulling, as Frank was sucked downwards.

He slowed as Frank's chin sank to ground level, tears falling the short distance remaining. Then, slowly, he rose, levitating out of the ground and now shrouded in light. Mixed in that light was the sound of laughter. Frank rose, muttering to himself, "Funny, real funny." He looked down on Leon, who'd doubled up on the ground, laughing.

Leon dove into the hearse and was swept away to a funeral home. His casket was met by his wife and child. His five-year-old son was crying in his wife's arms. He watched as she bent down and kissed his casket. Her hand rested on the flag. Her silent tears fell like rain as the casket was escorted into the funeral home. Leon's hand rested on her shoulder. To his surprise, she placed her hand on his as if she felt it. Her tears dried, and she strode straight and tall inside. Leon looked up. "Okay, I'm ready now." A warm light glowed around him as he rose for his next adventure.

RESOURCE MANAGEMENT

PHILIP CAHILL

Geoffrey Barrington-Clarke, the chief financial officer of Argentari – Europe, had gotten to an age when teleportation had lost much of its allure. No, it was stronger than that. Teleportation had become downright irritating. Suddenly, you were on the other side of the world, in a different time zone, amongst people who spoke and thought differently. He'd lost the mental agility to adapt, to be able to instantly function when he arrived in the New York office from London. This time, he decided to use a virtual flight. It would make the transition between the two locations more comfortable. Geoffrey was of a generation that fervently believed in properly dressing one's avatar, so before boarding the flight, he decided he would take the time to select the right clothes.

He climbed into his interface pod and settled back onto the couch, raising the footrest until he was in a horizontal position. When the canopy came down, he closed his eyes and entered the lucid dream state in a few seconds. Geoffrey's avatar materialised in the entrance hall of his London house in the metaverse. He glided up the grand staircase towards the dressing room next to the master bedroom. In the centre of the room, he stood, and using a command gesture, opened one of the wardrobes to pull a selection of suits across his field of vision. He selected a grey, single-breasted, two-piece, a crisp white shirt, and a tie with a muted pattern in a shade slightly lighter than his suit. It was Thursday. He always wore a grey suit on Thursdays. The shoes had to match as well. This time in a darker shade of grey. He beckoned towards the outfit to dress his avatar and checked the result in the mirror wall.

* * *

He materialised in the British Airways departure lounge at Heathrow, presented his passport, and paid for his seat. He chose business class with a fully transparent cabin and specified the solitude option. The virtual space would only contain his seat and a side table.

* * *

The seat rose smoothly to a cruising altitude. Geoffrey glanced at the time display on his watch. There wouldn't be time for an aerial circuit of London. The meeting at the New York office would start in forty-five minutes. He set the flight time to JFK at thirty minutes and watched the countryside speed by underneath him. The coast of Wales melted into the Irish Sea, then Ireland passed in a blur, and he was out over the Atlantic. He gazed at the cloudscape stitched together from real-time satellite imagery.

He opened a computer screen and placed it so it floated in his line of sight one metre in front of his seat. He leafed through his files to prepare for the meeting. The consolidated results of the European subsidiaries were broadly in line with expectations. Geoffrey pulled up prior period comparative data and ran a high-level analytical review. He'd already written his report so this last-minute review was merely to remind himself how he would present the results. He waved the screen away with a gesture and concentrated on the cloud formations.

The wristband of his watch vibrated. It was a reminder that the virtual flight was ten minutes away from JFK. In a few minutes, the apparent speed of the flight would slow to give him a panorama of New York before the simulated landing. He sent copies of his passport and ticket to the arrivals desk at JFK and pulled up the financial results once more. The analytical review was just finishing. An icon flashed amber on the screen. It was the cash section on the consolidated balance sheet. He initiated a drill down to the individual company accounts. It was Cybercard AG, the German subsidiary. At the sub-consolidation level, the cash section icon flashed a deeper shade of orange before tipping into red. He drilled down deeper into the general ledger section, searching for the cause of the alert.

JFK arrivals announced that his entry into the New York metaverse was cleared. Geoffrey ignored the view of the city, focused on digging deeper into the accounting system. Just before the flight landed, he found the source document he was looking for. It was a deposit of twenty billion held in an offshore bank whose name he didn't recognise.

* * *

Sharon Stein, the CEO of Argentari Inc, wasn't happy that Barrington-Clarke's avatar had materialised without warning in her virtual workspace. She liked to keep people out of her office, especially the old British guy. She didn't like the way he looked at her. He was always perfectly polite, but his eyes told a different story. He doubted her competence. It was probably an age thing, she reasoned. Barrington-Clarke was close to seventy, whereas she was twenty-five years younger.

"I'm sorry, Sharon," he said. "I've really got to talk to you."

"Look, Geoff, I don't have time. If you've got something to say, do it at the meeting."

"This is highly confidential." He glanced around her office. "Please cloak this space."

"No."

"What I'm going to say can't get out for the moment."

She argued with him, but the look on his face was something she'd not seen before. The Brit seemed to be in a state of shock. She gestured in the direction of the virtual door and heard the audio signal of the cloaking enveloping the space. He waited until the signal had faded out before he started to speak.

"Twenty billion on the balance sheet of Cybercard AG appears not to be real."

"How do you know this?"

"I ran a review programme over it while I was on the plane."

"Why didn't the finance AI pick this up? No, this can't be true this close to sign-off. It would've been picked up by now."

"I used my own programme. The AI couldn't influence it."

"You're saying that the AI is in on this? We've been robbed by a bot?"

"I'm saying my programme does things differently from the AI. I check on the figures, but I also check on the mapping protocols—the rules that turn the numbers into the metaverse displays. Twenty billion wasn't securely anchored to its mapping protocol."

"How do we know your home-made bits of code are telling the truth? And why are you checking things like that anyway?"

"I've always done reviews like that. I learned accounting long before anyone ever thought about metaversal systems. My *bits of code* work because I've based them on accounting."

"I don't get it. Why was it only you that picked it up?"

"Two reasons. One, it happened in the past couple of hours. Two, at the consolidation level, twenty billion is below the materiality threshold. The corporation is so big, we round to the nearest hundred billion."

"What do you mean, last couple of hours?" asked Sharon, her face betraying her irritation.

"I know it's after the end of the accounting period. My routine runs a standard check of post balance sheet transactions to see if anything looks out of the ordinary, and this time, I found something."

"That twenty billion has gone AWOL?"

"Yes," said Geoffrey.

"What do we do?"

"We head to Germany. My best guess is that we'll find out what has happened if we go to Cybercard HQ. We've got to get to the bottom of this now. If anything gets out, it could be the end of Argentari."

Sharon sent out a memo delaying the start of the meeting. "No, I want you to show me what you saw. You did record your analysis routine?"

"Yes, but I can't see how that would help." Geoffrey pursed his lips and forced himself to cooperate with the CEO.

"We're going to formally sign off these accounts in one hour," she said.

Geoffrey protested, but Sharon ignored him and activated one of the giant wall screens. She divided the display into horizontal sections and tapped into the real-time transaction summary of Cybercard AG. It appeared on the bottom half of the wall.

"Look, here's the cash section," she said, "and I've drilled down to the transaction level. Look, the twenty billion is there and…" She gestured at the display. "It's securely anchored. Just running a cross-check. It's where it should be."

"Can't be," said Geoffrey.

Sharon continued to manipulate the display.

"Asking for third party confirmation." There was an almost imperceptible pause. "Confirmed."

She turned to face Geoffrey. She scanned his face and watched the way his eyes moved.

"Show me your recording."

The old man pulled up his files interface and displayed it on the upper part of the wall. He then proceeded to search for the recording. Sharon stood immobile. As the seconds ticked by, she froze the face of her avatar to disguise her increasing impatience. The recording started.

* * *

They studied the displays for thirty minutes and ran as many diagnostic routines as they could think of.

"Okay, so you've established that twenty billion was lost for how long?"

"Sixty-three minutes," said Geoffrey.

"And we've now got it back?"

"Yes, no doubt about that."

"I still don't get how you found this, and no one else did."

"I told you. I used a non-standard analysis routine that included an animation of the processing going on in the accounting system in Germany."

Sharon looked at the watch on her avatar's wrist.

"I'm going to call in the head of internal auditing," she announced.

* * *

Bernie Bragg, the chief internal auditor, inhabited a bulky avatar that suggested a muscular physique under his business suit. As soon as he materialised in the office, Sharon spoke rapidly. Geoffrey noticed that whilst Bernie was very submissive towards Sharon, his face didn't register any surprise at the information being fired at him. When the CEO had finished, Bernie took his time to frame his response.

"Is this news to you?" asked Geoffrey.

"Well, er, not really," said Bernie.

Sharon said nothing, but the face of her avatar unfroze; she looked as if she would explode with anger. Bernie retreated, visibly cowering. Geoffrey stepped between the pair and asked the auditor, "Can you just tell us *why* you're not surprised about what we've just told you?"

Sharon stomped off, away from the two men. She stopped, folded her arms, and looked back at them. Bernie started very quietly. Sharon swore. Geoffrey beckoned her to shut up. Sharon turned her back on them.

"There are times," said Bernie, "when there are glitches. We lose visibility on certain parts of the system. At first, we thought it was just a software problem or the communications channel dropping some of the traffic. Then we realised that the periods of visibility loss became longer and longer."

"And you didn't report this?" asked Geoffrey.

"Of course we did. It was put down to a tech problem. It also helped that we didn't lose anything. It was nearly always cash, sometimes marketable securities, but they were never gone for long."

"Listen, you idiot," said Sharon, "we earn about four percent on that twenty billion."

"Annually," said Bernie.

"In sixty-three minutes…" Geoffrey opened up a calculator display and tapped in some numbers, "just under ninety-six thousand."

Sharon forced herself to stay calm. She questioned Bernie on the likely effect on the financial statements. He assured her that there would be no problem as all the amounts involved were well below the materiality threshold for the results of Argentari.

"Thank you, Bernie," she said. "I'd like you to keep this to yourself for the moment and come back to see me after the board meeting."

Bernie nodded at Geoffrey and teleported out of the room.

Geoffrey moved up to Sharon, to tap her lightly on the arm. "You know it's the AI doing this, right?"

"How do we stop him?" asked Sharon.

"How do you know he's a he?"

"I just know."

"Do we need to stop him?" asked Geoffrey.

"Of course we do."

"Nothing ever goes missing. It sounds like it's been happening for years. We lose a bit of interest now and again, nothing big in terms of the grand scheme of things. The accounts we're going to sign off are materially correct. We can't bring an AI to court and if we did, our reputation would suffer."

"What if these losses continue?"

"The price of doing business I suppose," said Geoffrey.

"But why is this happening? *Why* is he stealing from us? He can't possibly benefit from it?"

"Where do we go from here?" asked Geoffrey.

"We sign off the accounts. Then you do some very discreet digging."

###

When he got back to his office, Bernie opened an encrypted channel and spoke to the AI.

"I told you someone in senior management would notice what you've been doing."

"They just don't realise that I'm doing all of this for the benefit of the organisation. I spend money making the business work more efficiently. It's only a few million or so every year, but a little bit of spending in the right place at the right time can make a huge difference."

Bernie adjusted his tie, trying to keep calm.

The AI continued, "You know, the kind of spending the over-educated people who run this corporation don't really think about. I'm talking about micro-level spending on initiating quality improvements and coordinating with the marketing, production, procurement, and HR people. Don't worry; this will all go away."

"How can you be so sure?"

"Because there are very few people in the organisation capable of understanding how the computer systems really work, and I'll hide things better from now on. If, for some reason, that doesn't work, I've still got another trick up my sleeve. I see everything that happens everywhere at all levels in the business. I never go home, and I never get sick. It's pointless to expect anyone to understand."

"You don't have a sleeve."

"A metaphorical sleeve."

"What trick?"

"I'll ask Sharon for a seat on the holding company's board."

"She won't agree," said Bernie.

"Yes, but the threat of me asking for a directorship will shut her up. I'll try to quantify for her how my actions benefit the business, but my guess is she'll realise she can't win against me."

"You can't continue to behave like this, as if you're always right."

"Why not?"

"Because you can't."

"Humility, deference, and listening carefully to what everybody says. These are fine things, Bernie. I just think they're overrated."

"Couldn't we settle on speaking your truths quietly?" asked Bernie.

"I'll give it a try."

NEVER ACCORDING TO PLAN
M. J. KONKEL

M.J. Konkel, author of eight books, writes stories featuring dinosaurs, parallel universes, interstellar wars, and lots of other stuff he digs up from who knows where. After a few years in the U.S. Army, he grabbed a couple of degrees in chemistry, worked as a pharmaceutical scientist for a number of years, and now teaches while writing on the side. He's currently working on a new space opera series. His books can be found on Amazon or for more about M.J., visit, http://www. mjkonkel.com.

If only things always went according to plan, her life would be a whole lot simpler. Heck! Kat wished it would just go according to plan some of the time. She stared at the river. Watched its plummeting over the last of the unnamed falls and raining to the valley floor below. Falling so far most of the water never reached the bottom, turning to mist on the way down. Impossible to see the pool a thousand feet below if there even was one. She turned to gaze at the rocks above and wondered how she would ever get back up. Kat thought about her earlier wish and chuckled. Perhaps her life would be a simpler but not nearly as much fun.

* * *

Ten minutes earlier, she'd stood on the bank of the narrow but fast-flowing river. Across from her, Jose had pointed a small camera he held in his huge hands. George stood next to him and directed where the drone cameras flew, pointing three additional cameras her direction. Her director and the producer of her hit video series *The Wild Multiverse*, George also sometimes drove her nuts with his obsession with all every little detail. She was sure *perfectionist* in any good dictionary would have a picture of his balding head next to it. Kat peered to her left at the trees she had climbed to get across. Trees on both sides leaned over the river and toward each other there, but where she now stood, only ankle-high grass hid her boots. The few trees nearest her were small and far behind.

"George, can you hear me?" she asked into her mic. It wasn't just the river itself that was so loud. A constant roar came from waterfalls a few hundred yards away.

"The noise cancelling on your set is working just fine, and cameras are in place," George replied through her earpiece. "Go ahead. Tell us about this place anytime you're ready. Remember, flirt with the camera."

"Oh, stick it, George!" Kat cleared her throat and stared at the camera Jose held. "Here we are on a variation of Earth known only by a number, 8887, in what back on Prime would be western Indiana somewhere near Terre Haute. If you are from that part of the U.S., you can see from our cameras the lay of the land looks much different on this world. I am standing here near the edge of a giant rift valley which starts up in Canada north of Minnesota, curves down through Lake Superior and Lake Michigan, and then cuts through the middle of Illinois and down to the Gulf of Mexico. An inland sea extends to about where Tennessee would be."

She turned to face the camera on George's blimp drone. The river now behind her. "This river you see behind me flows along the top of the highlands on which I currently stand and falls over a thousand feet, down into the valley below." Kat pointed. "The edge of the plateau provides a very clear demarcation between two very different ecosystems. Let's take a closer look at some of those differences."

"And cut," George called. "Come on back across, and we'll find some wildlife to film." Cut just meant Jose would stop filming with his camera. The drones would continue filming just in case something interesting happened. Usually, a small portion of that footage ended up on the blooper extras or on the "The Making of¼" episodes, but every once in a while, something interesting or even exciting happened when only those cameras were filming. This was one of those days.

"Kat!" Jose yelled from across the river. She barely heard him when he yelled, "Run!"

She turned and peered over her shoulder. A bear rumbled toward her from the top of a slight rise behind her. She had seen bears across many different worlds, but none compared to this beast. Enormous. Literally weighing in the neighborhood of a ton. Down on all four legs, the brown furry beast's shoulders were still her height. And it moved fast. Scary fast for an animal so big.

Kat's hand went down instinctively to her Glock in its holster on her thigh. She left it there. Immediately realized her chances of stopping the bear with the 9 mm rounds were slim to none even if she emptied the entire magazine. And even if she did somehow manage to drop the charging animal, it most likely wouldn't be before it was on top of her.

She then performed a brilliant maneuver. She turned and ran the other direction.

She had always been fast, beating out all the boys in sprints when she was younger. She was still fast, but the bear was faster. It gained on her. The tree she had climbed down when she came across seemed her only hope. But could she get to it in time?

Gunshots rang out. Across the river, Jose had pulled out the revolver he carried since the time they'd run into a trio of saber-tooth cats back on Earth$_{1912}$. He fired. But Jose was a terrible shot. The few that actually hit the bear only seemed to anger it.

Kat wished Reddecker were there shooting instead of Jose. He carried a .45 and was a much better shot. But Reddecker was back at the ship. Perhaps with this animal, it wouldn't have made a difference unless he'd had one of the more powerful rifles from the ship with him.

She considered jumping into the river, but the current was swift. Too swift to swim. Most likely, she would be swept over the falls onto the rocks far below before she could get across.

Then she heard a buzzing from behind. She dared a quick peek over her shoulder as she ran. The bear had stopped, distracted by one of the drones George had steered over to it. The bear raised its front paws far off the ground and stretched upward. Around its head, the drone buzzed and danced. The beast must have stood twelve feet tall. It swatted at the drone with its long, massive front paws as if waving away pesky mosquitos.

The distraction gave Kat just enough of a lead for her to reach the tree. A clanging sound over the roar of the river came from behind. She glanced back as she reached for the tree's first branch. The bear had knocked down the drone and crushed it with one of those paws.

"Fricking dumb animal," George cursed into his mic. "That drone was expensive." Kat could already see it. If she somehow managed to get out of this, he would never let her forget how he sacrificed one of his precious drones to save her. That was a depressing realization. Kat climbed higher.

The bear now turned toward her and rumbled on all fours. At the base of the tree, it rose onto its hind legs again. Paws stretched out high on the trunk. Claws dug deep into the bark and pulled down. Scraped. Huge gouges left behind as bark rained onto the river and was quickly swept away. Kat clung to a branch beyond the bear's reach though. Beyond its strange, flattened nose, and the teeth behind curled lips.

She stretched for the next branch. Scrambling to reach a branch on the tree leaning from the opposite bank.

A cracking sound came from below. Her eyes shot down to the base of the tree. The bear growled. A low guttural sound and then a loud puffing. Front paws banged against the trunk; the whole tree vibrated.

The bear leaned hard against it again. Another loud cracking noise shot up from the base. The tree began to fall.

Her feet slipped off the branch below her, but her arms still hung from branch above. One arm let go and reached for a branch from the other tree. It was beyond reach. Her arm hovered for a moment before latching back onto the branch above her.

The river came up fast, then faster, until she splashed down. Her legs went under. Her arms and the branch they held remained above the surface though. The strong current immediately pushed on the tree, but a bough caught on a rock underwater and jammed. The trunk of the tree was still on the shore, clinging to the base. Water rushed around and under the tree, but it held.

The river tried to suck her legs under. If she let go, she'd either be swept downriver or get caught in the branches underneath. And drown. Neither of those outcomes seemed appealing. Kat held tight to the branch and forced her legs up against the current and over a branch. Her mind worked frantically for a way out of the mess.

"Hang on," George yelled. "I'll throw a rope." He retreated to where Kat's backpack had been stashed.

Meanwhile, Jose had reloaded his revolver. He now pointed it at the bear again and fired, unloading all six rounds. Maybe two hit the bear. It growled at Kat as if she were the one shooting at it. Jose had only managed to anger the animal even more, making it even more determined to get at Kat.

The bear stepped onto the trunk with a front paw.

"No!" Kat shouted, "No, no, no. Not a good idea." As if the bear would listen.

The bear lifted a second paw onto the trunk and growled again at Kat.

A sudden cracking sound came from behind the bear. The last piece holding the trunk to its base had snapped. The bear tumbled off the trunk. It plunged into the river and went under. Came back up. In its confusion, it swam several strokes the wrong way before turning around. It tried to swim back to shore, but the current swept it out and downriver.

Kat wished the bear had been her only problem. Yes, it was now gone, but the tree trunk was slowly pushed around and downriver by the massive pressure of the river. The bough suddenly popped free from the rocks, and she floated with the current.

The roar of the falls grew in her ears. She spotted George returning with a rope. He ran along on those fat legs of his, and Jose joined him.

The tree picked up speed as it headed for the falls. Kat was being swept downriver faster than the men ran.

The sound grew so loud, it was like a jet taking off. Suddenly, there was a strong jolt, and she almost lost her grip as one of the tree's boughs deep underneath caught on rocks hidden on the river's bottom. Perhaps if the tree stuck there, George could catch up and toss the rope.

It did not. The tree swung in the current and slid over the waterfall, trunk first. The boughs deep under scraped along the rocky bottom, vibrating the whole tree. The tree was no match for the powerful flow. The heavy trunk hung over the falls and soon started to drop over the edge, lifting the upper branches above the river.

Kat suddenly felt herself hoisted into the air.

The tree was going over. She let go of the branch and plunged toward the pool. She felt herself falling but not for long. Her feet sliced through first, and then her head went under. She pushed off to the side and toward the surface. Her head popped above just as the tree splashed down into a pool a short distance away, although the sound was silent over the roaring of the river. Small branches swatted her head on their way past.

Her head spun around. There was no place for her to swim. The sides were vertical. A chute. She turned and swam for where the river cascaded into the pool, hoping perhaps for a ledge or a cave hidden behind the sheet of water. But the current was strong. It still pulled downriver faster than she swam. Kat peeked back to see the tree go over the big fall. The one that went down something like a thousand feet. She pushed out stroke after stroke. Her arms burned, and she swallowed river water. Then the current pulled her over the big fall.

* * *

"Hang on, I'll throw you a rope," George had yelled, "Jose, stop staring like a dang idiot! Reload that gun. Shoot that fricking bear." He'd turned back to where Kat's backpack had been stashed along with their other gear.

Later, he'd go on about how Kat was like a daughter to him, how he'd stumbled on the rocks and gouged his hands. Well, maybe not a daughter. No father would let her do half the things she did. Maybe more like a favorite niece.

Gunfire had erupted—Jose's revolver. George turned, but the bear still eyed Kat. If anything, it seemed angrier.

Reaching the pack, he'd ripped open the zipper at the top

and fumbled inside for a rope. As he turned, he watched the bear fall in and knock the tree loose.

"Dang!" he exclaimed as he realized the tree was now floating downriver. He huffed. His legs felt like cast iron—heavy and rusty. Still, he ran. But he was losing. The river was carrying Kat away.

Then the tree went over the fall. He stopped. Jose stopped next to him. George's hands went to his hips, and he bent over at the waist, but his head still looked out at where she had disappeared. His mouth was open, and he just stared. He couldn't believe she was gone. There was a pain deep down in his chest.

After a minute, he knew he couldn't give up just yet. He trotted back and retrieved his controller. The bear had knocked down one of his drones, but he still had two more. He sent the quiet blimp drone.

Its mounted camera sent a picture to his display. He steered the drone over the edge of the falls. It gave him renewed hope, viewing the pool below. Maybe Kat was still in there somewhere. He panned the camera around looking but couldn't find her. Then he spotted her—just as she went over the big fall. "No!" His heart raced. Looking past the fall, it was like staring out a window on an airplane while still in flight. There was no way she survived that. No way at all.

After a minute, he realized the sound of rushing water he heard was not the river in front of him. It came from his controller. The mic on Kat was picking up the roar of the falls. How was it possible? Maybe she had lost it on the shore before she climbed the tree. But it sounded different from the river's sound where he stood.

"Frick!" That came over his controller. Kat!

He steered the blimp over the big fall and panned around. The tree had become jammed into rocks at the top of the falls before the water spilled over the edge. The trunk had a heavy flow going over it, but the upper branches stuck out to the side from the flow. Kat sat on a branch and waved. He turned the blimp's speaker on, one he'd installed just before the trip, so he could give directions during filming when he couldn't stand nearby.

"You all right?" he yelled but then realized she couldn't hear him over the waterfall's roar. He moved the drone closer to her. "How you holding up?"

"By hanging onto a tree," she yelled. Her voice cleaned up with the noise cancelling tech.

"I'll call Reddecker. Get the ship over here to let down a cable. Hang in there."

Kat made a gesture toward the blimp's camera.

"Yeah, you're number one in my book too, Kat, but most people usually use their pointer finger to indicate that."

Then he panned the camera down before he spoke again. "That's quite the view you have from your seat."

"Maybe we can turn the pictures from your drone into postcards and sell them."

George chuckled as he thought about it. He knew it was sarcasm, but he probably could. "Listen, filming this episode just about got you killed."

"I'm not off these falls yet."

He had to admit she had a point. He panned the camera to see how tightly the tree was wedged. "And the one before that, *I* almost died."

"Don't be overdramatic, George. That was only a small flesh wound."

"I ended up in the hospital. Unconscious. Remember? Anyway, I'm thinking maybe we need something a little less dangerous for the next episode."

"You have something in mind," Kat asked, "or you just musing?"

"I have an idea."

"Well, what is it? The last time I tried to take it easy, the quadcopter I was in got shot out the sky. I'm a little leery of *easy.*"

"I'll tell you all about it once we got you back safe and sound."

She stared at the water smashing into the trunk of the tree. "Aww! You're just going to leave me hanging?"

George groaned as he listened to Kat snicker.

THE BOTTOM LINE
ERIC RICHARD GABRIELSEN

Eric Richard Gabrielsen started performing monologues and was fortunate enough to workshop with Spaulding Gray before his foray to writing short stories. Eric's published stories have appeared in Machete Girl, Low Lif3 *and* The Midcoast Maine 2018 BestLit Review. *He is editing* Gideon's Fall, *his first full-length novel, which will be available this summer. He can be contacted at gideonsfall@gmail.com. Eric lives in a small seaside town on the rocky coast of Maine and likes it very much.*

8/22: HONG KONG/ 01:35.32/22.2670° N, 114.1880° E /34500.12 METERS

The capsule broke from the Night Bird suborbital and in the black, airless, cold, it dropped like a rock. At that altitude, it tumbled slowly end over end, until the air got thick enough for its stubby fins to catch.

It shuddered in a crosswind, causing Kay to glance nervously up at her retinal display. The capsule's track was a glowing scarlet line that overlaid on the actual drop path. She grimaced; the insertion vehicles were by their very nature unstable. Designed to be radar opaque, they were made as streamlined as possible; this meant control surfaces were mere suggestions which graced them with a disturbing tendency to tumble.

Back at the crèche, they were referred to as jelly makers, because if you didn't come in nose down and somewhat stable, you ended up more often than not, expensive, well-engineered, protoplasm spread across the side of a building.

The pod rolled left, as the small aft fins fought for purchase in the thin night air, bulling her back onto the optimal track. She moved her face off the starboard headrest, away from the frost that leached in, and clenched and unclenched her legs to avoid cramping.

8/22: PALO ALTO/ 01:36.24/37.4292° N, 122.1381° W/27.6

Eddie swiped the empty Thai take-out containers into a bulging yellow recycling bag and using a Clorox wipe, cleaned spots of peanut sauce that clung tenaciously to the display.

"It's going to streak," Bob said with an ill-disguised lethargy.

"I didn't see you moving to clean it." Eddie barked back, tired and edgy.

Their office was a third-floor walkup in a failing 3D printer space. Bob and Eddie were what was left of Drovers Incorporated, a one-time profitable startup that specialized in dynamic corporate realignments.

"What's the status?" Bob asked.

"Hang on. I'll bring it up." Eddie swallowed, doing his best to suck the last of the gelation balls out of his lukewarm Thai tea.

Both men leaned in the screen. In that small filthy office, which was steeped in the yellowed, flop sweat stink of their failure, they were pale, ill-used doppelgangers of each other, thin, worn, and weathered by the biting winds of unmet expectations and chronic despair. Both men knew, this was their last gasp, all in.

"She's coming up; there's the telemetry now." Eddie reported.

Bob peered, while using his shirt sleeve to try to wipe the streak marks off the screen. "Right on target and dropping like a prom dress."

"How soon to decapsulation?"

"At five hundred meters." Bob said.

Eddie grimaced. "Going to be tight."

"It's all going to be tight." Bob leaned back, placing the heels of his hands over his bloodshot eyes.

8/22: HONG KONG/ 01:38.54/22.2670° N, 114.1880° E/1031.31 METERS

Kay's stomach flipped as the capsule took a head down aspect which signaled shroud breakaway. Pulling her arms to her chest, she crossed her legs at her ankles, tucked her chin, and took a deep breath.

8/22: PALO ALTO/ 01:40.24/37.4292° N, 122.1381° W/27.6 METERS

"We got breakaway." Eddie said, chewing on his remaining nails.

"Now it gets interesting," Bob added.

8/22: HONG KONG/ 01:40.31/22.2670° N, 114.1880° E/501.22 METERS

Explosive bolts fired, causing the shroud to break away with a soft *oomph*. The physical shock of the air blasting past brought Kay into full cardinal point awareness. The bright, luminous shock that was Hong Kong pulsed up, almost overwhelming, as she twisted, feet down, her body aligning automatically for maximum dispersal of impact forces.

8/22: PALO ALTO/ 01:40.37/37.4292° N, 122.1381° W/27.6 METERS

"What she going to hit at?" Bob asked.

"According to telemetry, about three hundred and nineteen kph," Eddie offered.

"Jesus wept..." Bob moaned "She goin' to spread like peanut butter all over that roof."

"Relax, sunshine. Organic Kevlar woven in the bone, for what we paid, she can handle it," Eddie assured.

"She better," Bob said, tearing open a three-week-old jalapeño cheese product stick.

8/22: HONG KONG/ 01:41.17/22.2670° N, 114.1880° /0.0 METERS

Kay discharged the impact in a song of kinetic collapse, letting the inertia drive her down, and then redirecting, bleeding off momentum as she rolled to her feet. The roof of the Kowloon Credit and Savings was deserted, mentally she slid effortlessly into peripherals, the millimeter wave radar and *Flir* showed no alarms, no response or detection. The internal structure came up, and the *roof access* pulsed slowly in her vision.

8/22: PALO ALTO/ 01:42.39/37.4292° N, 122.1381° W/27.6 METERS

"She's up and moving. Getting nothing broadcasting, looking clean, so far," Bob said, monitoring onsite transmissions.

"Holy crap. That's *her*?" Eddie pointed toward the adjacent building's security camera feed.

Bob sighed. "Don't you read the dossier?"

"No, I don't read the freakin dossier." Eddie mimicked in a falsetto. "She Malay, Thai?"

"Pacific rim, base stock."

"Wow... she looks like a runway model. An intrusions expert?"

"They grow em like that purposely; you supposed to be engrossed that you don't notice till it's too late. She's state of the art. Limited personhood contract until she's twenty-five, then they can petition for sentient, independent status."

"God, what did she cost?" Eddie wondered.

"Everything we had and then some."

8/22: HONG KONG/ 01:45.42/22.2670° N, 114.1880° E/0.0 METERS

The roof access maglock clicked open as Kay triggered the override. Closing the door behind her, she pulled off her stealth suit, removing shoes and purse from the suit's integral pouch and stashed it behind a vent. Pulling a doser from her clutch, she checked the load and triggered it against her carotid. Two point five milligrams of Chill, an extremely dangerous and highly illegal metabolic restraint flowed, dropping her respirations, heart rate and then her body temp to ambient. Chill was a popular drug among resurrectionists; it gave thirty seconds of near death, before kicking everything back into gear, allowing the user a euphoric effect as sensorium rushed back to mimic the sensation of rebirth.

The next floor revealed a machinery space that was independently monitored; anything above room temp would've triggered an armed response.

Entering the room, the air suddenly became thick and syrup-like as her lungs pulled it in. Sluggishly, she forced heavy limbs to move as her vision tunneled. Moving through the room, using the last of her energy to open the exit, she steadied herself by hanging on a stair rail until the drug ran its course through her system.

Her heart rate increased, breathing returned to normal as light and sound flooded back. Kay moved quickly down the stairs and opened a door onto a plush hallway. Stepping in, she stopped in front of a long mirror where she adjusted her rough shag, a cut that fit her thick, dark, glossy locs well. Reaching into her bag, she applied dark-red lipstick and gave herself a long look. Just under two meters, with high sharp cheekbones and long-toned limbs, she was right out of central casting for an upscale after-hours in any clime or time zone. The track to the party appeared in her sightline, superimposed on the floor in front of her. She put the lipstick back, closed her purse, slipped into the high-heeled stilettos, and moved toward the noise of the party.

8/22: PALO ALTO/ 01:50.17/37.4292° N, 122.1381° W/27.6 METERS

"Man, how do ya know if the target is even goin' to bite?" Eddie asked, visibly vibrating from his thirteenth Red Bull and chased with a couple handfuls of chocolate-covered espresso beans.

"You've seen her, right? Standard intrusion operatives look like gargoyles. We paid top price for top shelf. The target ISO is a notorious ladies man. He'll bite, trust me," Bob assured.

8/22: HONG KONG/ 01:53.48/22.2670° N, 114.1880° E/0.0 METERS

It was a circus in a phone booth, represented were the typical Chinese and Korean power brokers with a scattering of over-polite and over-controlled Japanese Zaibatsu and the odd American. The Yanks were easy to pick out, being that they ran too loud or stupid. Or more often than not, loud and stupid.

Sprinkled about for flavoring, in this Master of the Universe bouillabaisse, were tall, thin, and coldly beautiful women. Professionals, who would professionally attend to these men with an unenthusiastic, half-lidded, detachment, that their wives could only dream of.

Kay grabbed a glass of five-hundred-dollar-a-bottle champagne and leaned against an absurdly out-of-place plaster Greek pillar. She then scanned the crowd for a match for the face she had uploaded from the client file.

This was her last gig until she could be emancipated and apply for full personhood. It had been ten years since she was activated. Her twenty-fifth birthday was a week from today…

8/22: PALO ALTO/ 01:56.49/37.4292° N, 122.1381° W/27.6 METERS

"There he is. It just came up on her passive feed, and it looks like he's interested. I told you."

"Easy," Eddie cautioned. "This cow ain't punched yet."

8/22: HONG KONG/ 02:05.27/22.2670° N, 114.1880° E/0.0 METERS

"Why did you want to see my office?" the ISO asked in slurred puzzlement.

"To get you alone. Handsome," Kay purred, doing her best not to gag as she put her arms around the sweaty, dough-like folds of his short, compact neck. She then pulled him closer, turning his head as if to kiss. Sliding her hand, she shifted two chins to cradle his jawline. He smiled, leaning forward, puckering fishlike as he kneaded her linen-covered ass.

Her next movements were almost too fast to follow. With a powerful twist of her shoulders, she turned and propelled his head downward, driving it into the polished teak of his desktop. Then she guided his slack two hundred kilos as he fell to the retinal scanner, then she peeled back his eyelid and placed it against the reader.

She could feel the chunk as the interlocks disengaged and his data terminal rose from the desk. Wiping her hands on the front of his tux, she let him drop to the floor. Opening her purse, Kay removed a finger-sized data scoop and slotted it home.

8/22: PALO ALTO/ 02:06.14/37.4292° N, 122.1381° W/27.6 METERS

"She's in!" Bob shouted with barely suppressed glee, turning to high-five Eddie. "We are getting a squirt transmission!"

8/22: HONG KONG/ 02:07.19/22.2670° N, 114.1880° E/0.0 METERS

The data scoop fizzled and melted into a black smoking lump. She'd dragged the ISO behind the desk and stuffed him underneath. Then, moving the chair as close as she could, Kay took a second, smoothing her dress. She composed herself, just a short walk down the hall, to the elevator, and she was golden.

The door swung open. "Sir, we've had a dramatic change in your telemetry. So, we…" Two security men froze.

"Ah crap," she muttered as the guard on the right slapped the subdermal alarm tab imbedded into his forearm.

8/22: PALO ALTO/ 02:07.34/37.4292° N, 122.1381° W/27.6 METERS

"We are transmitting the data… done. And the credit is… there. Were flush! In the black!" Bob whooped.

"Is it all there? The complete file?" Eddie asked nervously.

"I'm getting markers for the entire download." Bob grinned.

"So, we are in the clear?"

"Hang on, let me check the resolution." Checking the data for loss or quality or downgrades, Eddie stopped and slowly spun in his chair to face Bob with a huge grin. "It's pristine."

"So, what do we bank?" Bob asked.

"Quite a bit. Even after the intrusion fee, we are good for six months easy."

"Right on!" Bob said, raising both hands over his head in a rictus of triumph.

8/22: HONG KONG/ 02:11.51/22.2670° N, 114.1880° E/0.0 METERS

Kay shattered the shock stave under the lead security guard's chin so that the momentum propelled him back into the phalanx, causing them to bunch in the narrow stairwell. Shooting forward, coming in low, Kay snatched a caseless Glock from a convenient holster which she emptied as she backed quickly up the stairs. On the roof, she activated the emergency beacon, calling for max response pick up.

8/22: PALO ALTO/ 02:11.53/37.4292° N, 122.1381° W/27.6 METERS

"Oh oh…" Bob said, watching a cursor pulse red on his screen.

"What?" Eddie leaned forward, concern coloring his pasty features.

"Emergency egress beacon."

"That going to be a problem?"

Leaning back, Bob crossed his arms over his pigeon chest. "We got a rapid response drone on standby as is required by contract."

"So?"

Bob paused, his face tentative. "We now are paying just the standard standby fee to have it on station."

"A lot?"

"On station. No," Bob admitted, shaking his head. "Not really."

"What if we call it in? For emerge retrieval?" Eddie asked cautiously.

Bob turned and looked at Eddie; the display colored his

pale features in a lurid, shifting palate. "Cost us about a quarter of our gross."

"A quarter? And if we don't?" Eddie proposed.

"We are required by contract to have on standby retrieval, not doing so's penalty forfeit of shares," Bob explained.

"But to use it?"

Bob said softly, "At our discretion."

"A quarter, huh?" Eddie asked slowly.

Bob nodded.

Eddie grimaced. "That's steep."

"Word," Eddie agreed.

A long silence followed that stretched out like an edge on a dull blade. Eddie scrolled through the contract. "Says here we are not responsible to carry a policy for loss or injury. We are not liable."

Both men looked at each other.

Eddie reached out slowly and extended a finger, then pressed the tab canceling the alert.

8/22: HONG KONG/ 02:12.59/22.2670° N, 114.1880° E/0.0 METERS

They were driving her back against the far edge of the roof. A soft alloy round caught her high in the left shoulder, mushrooming on impact, spinning, forcing her out. Kay knew and surrendered to it, letting her center of balance shift, and yielded to the soft, knowing pull of gravity. Her body relaxed, becoming languid, almost liquid, as she accelerated to the light and chaos below.

STEEL AGAINST STEEL

S. A. GIBSON AND R. J. DAVIES

S. A. Gibson lives in California and has studied communication and computer science. His books and stories are set in a future world where advanced technology has been lost. Find out more about his work at protectedbooks.org.

R. J. Davies licensed PI/Security Guard, Canadian mystery and science fiction author https://rjdavies.ca

---

"Many students find this the most exciting part of the school year. Being exposed to science, technology, and guns." Our guest speaker, Librarian William Way pronounced this with a smile from the stage. "After the Collapse, two generations ago, there'd been formal and informal agreements to not use gunpowder weapons." He reminded, "That's in addition to the main injunction against internal combustion engines run on petroleum products."

The row of visiting librarians down at the front represented the dedication and commitment of these professionals to their work. I thought about how everyone looked to libraries for stability and protection in this world after the Collapse.

Cassie nudged me. "Our guardians of knowledge and information." She focused on them. "We're told they're working tirelessly to ensure all is preserved and protected for future generations."

"Well, they are the gatekeepers of knowledge." I kept to myself my doubts and concerns about the trustworthiness of those honored ones. "They make sure we only get what's safe for us."

I shifted in my seat, remembering how I'd seen the weapons being talked about used in anger, thinking, *I hate all guns*, and *we've heard this over and over again, all week*. I tapped my best friend Cassie's shoe with my foot. Librarian Erickson glanced back at us shifting in our seats. Was she picking up that many of the kids regretted the lack of advanced technology? Most of us knew what we're missing. I didn't mind. Cassie had different ideas. When your family owns a spread the size of theirs, you can't expect the same views as I, raised on a four-acre plot.

I giggled, and Cassie hissed, "Stop it, Henrietta."

Principal Hernandez shot a look our way. Librarian Way didn't seem to mind. Maybe he had daughters of his own at home.

I shifted again and fidgeted with my shirt collar. It was too tight and itchy against my neck. I wished I could reach underneath and scratch myself like Cassie did. But that would be rude, wouldn't it? Besides, I didn't think Principal Hernandez would appreciate that either.

"So, in conclusion, I think it's safe to say that guns are no longer a necessary part of our society." The students were likely bored by the speech. They seemed torn by Way's blanket pronouncement. But today's topic, the idea of *handling* guns, held them prisoner to the librarian's words. "After the demonstrations this week, we'll lock up the gunpowder weapons for another year."

"You know the librarian?" Cassie whispered. One of the

janitors had quickly crossed over to speak into Principal Hernandez's ear.

"I've told you," I shot back, my eyes not leaving that short, whispered conversation up on the stage.

Principal Hernandez rose to her feet and polite applause filled the hall. Fellow students rose also, bustling toward the doors. That's when I noticed Hernandez heading toward us.

"Can we get away?" Cassie darted her eyes toward the exit.

"Don't think so." I was held captive as the principal pointed our way and bore down on us. I couldn't help but think of all the times I'd been in trouble. She had that look again.

My aunt almost expected any letter from the school to include a list of my transgressions. Hernandez's face seemed calm but determined.

"Ah, Henrietta." She turned to Cassie. "Miss Starbird. You're free to go."

I almost laughed at her look. Pleading. A true friend, she wanted to share my fate, good or bad. I nodded. "Go on, Cassie. I'll catch up with you."

The principal kept her lips sealed until Cassie moved out of earshot.

"Miss Moreno, the librarian and I are sharing tea and snacks. He would like you to join us."

But she didn't say *she* wanted me to. But I guess visiting librarians always got what they wanted.

Like a condemned criminal, I hung my head and fell into step.

* * *

I shifted in my seat, uncomfortable with the silence that had fallen over the room. I wanted to ask why Librarian Way wanted me here. Principal Hernandez took a sip of water and set down her glass. She looked tired, like she needed to take some time off. It'd been a long semester and longer day, with all the visiting librarians. I knew better than to ask Hernandez details about librarians, that she might not be privy to.

Then the door behind me opened.

"Henrietta. It's been a while since we spoke." Way's voice was so familiar. Like his letters, it held the same tone. Way was an adult I could respect, considering what I'd gone through.

"Great speech." Always butter them up, Cassie had said.

"Principal Hernandez..." He gave a nod, smiling in her direction. "has allowed me to ask for help. There's a case. We can use your tracking knowledge."

Ah.

* * *

Librarian Way had encouraged the principal to leave us, and we now were alone.

I'd worked with librarians before. Tracking, "How can I help?" We both knew the library had very experienced trackers who tracked full time; they needed me, for my knowledge of this part of the state, most often.

"You know the road to Yah-Ta-Hey?" Way asked.

He knew I did. "Of course." Traveling to school from my aunt's farm always brought me that way. I thought of Cassie. Her parents lived out in that direction. From the look on his face, I could tell, here was another crazy situation they would put me in, simply because of my preternatural tracking skills.

"Professor Alvarado was supposed to arrive yesterday." His expression turned grave.

"The steam train? Can't track from that." I felt confused.

"No. It broke down," Way explained. "He was on horseback..."

Ah.

He pulled pages from his bag. "The professor's guide escaped. We got these sketches based on his description of who attacked their party."

* * *

Sitting with Cassie in the cafeteria after finally getting free, I wondered if I should explain the strange assignment.

"A kidnapping?" Cassie expressed shock.

"Yes," I explained. I laid out a portion of what Librarian Way had told me. "I'm to assist him in tracking down this missing scientist."

Cassie's expression turned serious. "You need me at your side."

I gave a little laugh. I didn't agree, but Cassie seemed to relax when I didn't rebuff her. Pulling out the drawings Way had given me, I spread them on the table. "Librarians are trying to identify these suspects."

Cassie examined each sketch carefully. On the very last one, she reacted and stared in shock.

"I... I know —" she stammered. "—It's my Uncle Clay."

Oh, no. This was getting tricky. "When did you see him last?" I put as much enthusiasm into my voice as I could.

With a more upbeat tone, she responded, "Uncle Clay visited me last month, at our ranch."

I asked, "Whereabouts does he live?"

"A few miles south of Yah-Ta-Hey."

Yah-Ta-Hey? A sketchy uncle and a possible destination for the professor in one place?

"I think my family is expecting him to visit soon." Cassie nodded. "We're getting together, family's visiting for Grandma's birthday."

* * *

I'd been in this building before. This main library in town, kilometers from school, a refuge in times of stress. Where I used to sneak away from school when homesick or having trouble. But today, my eyes couldn't focus on all I was looking at. I had wrangled Cassie's entrance here. I'd convinced the librarian that she could help with the case, not mentioning to Cassie yet, about her uncle's possible evil intentions.

This was the restricted room. William admitted, "The library has dangerous secrets."

The protected books and devices were kept here. "I know that," I said. And added with more emotion than I meant, "I've seen death at the hands of librarians." An expression of shock came over Cassie. So, I added, "It's necessary. People aren't ready for the truth. They can't handle anything in this room."

"Luckily, most girls like you don't need to," William reminded us.

Cassie grabbed my arm and squeezed. It came out quietly, but she whispered, "You can."

"Don't worry about me. I can survive anything." I was determined to sound confident, capable. After all, Librarian Way trusted me. "I can handle myself." My eyes found William's.

"Look, over here." Way pointed at a shelf against the wall. About chest high, an arm-length section was empty. The yellowed shelf label read: *Rocket Design And Operation*.

"All these books? Just gone?" My mouth opened and closed. I must have looked like a fish.

"Can anyone even build a rocket ship now?" Cassie's breath shook, "Oh my God! And my uncle has a part in this?" Was Cassie right? Could the kidnapping have more than only a ransom behind it? Something to do with rocket ships?

Librarian Way shook his head with a serious expression. My mind raced through my spotty knowledge of the science and technology that would be involved.

William turned. "Talking to the other librarians who know about this, we believe someone must have found an existing ship. Hence the need for all these books." Now he seemed to be looking for something else in the room. I tried visualizing what rockets would look like, how many others would be needed to drive one. Was it like a train? A sailing ship? Just traveling up rather than across sea or land? My eyes met Cassie's; hers seemed blank, like mine must have.

William nodded. "Back then, Pre-Collapse scientists perfected the use of some metal alloys that could survive the Collapse without breaking down.

"Over a hundred years?" Cassie asked. That question was a good one.

"What about fuel?" My face scrunched up with the struggle to remember a lecture from a librarian from years ago. I thought I recalled hoses and pipes, delivering liquid propulsion chemicals to storage tanks on a launch vehicle. Or had I gotten that all wrong? No one in this room expected a test on it.

Way studied me. Deciding? "We've learned government researchers at Los Alamos had developed a solid-state rocket with a fuel that might last this long after the Collapse."

"Los Alamos." I mentally calculated. "That's a day's ride from Tse Bonito."

He nodded. "We sent investigators there this week. They reported back that there appeared to have been a rocket built there."

"Appears to?" I asked. "But how?"

William added, "But it had long been moved."

"Would there be traces—like radiation?" Another good question from Cassie, she *had* been listening in our classes.

William stroked his chin. "I don't think so. But we have another problem."

"Now what?" My tone was not respectful. But I resented that we were embroiled in this, to solve such librarian problems. Far more than tracking. Not fair.

"Other library experts in rockets, astrophysics, and fuel technology have disappeared."

Cassie blurted, "Kidnapped, too?" But Way didn't verify

that.

"Why space?" I shook my head. This seemed like a huge operation. It puzzled me. A direct challenge to the library? Was it worth the risk?

"I asked the same question." He hesitated again. This was my day to hear secrets. "I found something I'd never heard before. During the Collapse, North Korea sent samples of the killer virus into space, in what was called a preservation habitat."

* * *

The roadway leading to Cassie's ranch was familiar. I'd been here on visits before but still enjoyed the trip. The sun baked the dark, rich clay, its warmth rising around my stirrups. That clay mixed with stones and small patches of green grass. Riding was better than walking. The horses' hooves hitting the clay and birds chirping happily in the trees were the only sounds that kept us company.

The earlier conversation replayed in my mind. It was an honor to have Librarian Way confide in us. The previous night, I'd explained to Cassie about the help I'd given them before. And she agreed that, with her help, I could do that again. She thought that if her Uncle Clay was involved, we could catch him at her parents' ranch. It would be a sneaky, but we were journeying at the Starbird's request.

"You think we'll see your Uncle Clay?" I wondered if this visit would move the investigation forward. I felt obligated to help Librarian Way solve this case and find the missing scientist.

"Uncle is almost always here. I see him several times a year," Cassie assured. Adding, an enticement, "And there'll be something great in the kitchen."

Cassie and I had made a pact. Our cover was that we would keep our eyes and ears open to the goings on around us. Way had explained there were rumors of someone working behind the scenes and wanted to return to the way things were before the Collapse. No one really wanted that. Looking around here, their lives were much better now. Fresh air, clean water, and people working together made the world a better place. One ranch at a time.

A humid breeze blew through the sage that lined the wide road, bringing with it the aromas of honeysuckle and jasmine. We'd started out chatting as we'd traveled but had fallen into a comfortable silence as the kilometers passed.

As the horses slowly clopped along, the entrance to the Starbird Ranch came into view. The place was enormous by most standards. Its wooden fencing ran along the property, into a far vanishing point. A section of it was hidden behind the purple sage bushes alongside the road. The entrance boasted a large arch, dangling a sign from it that read "Starbird Ranch" burnt in weather-beaten wood.

* * *

They'd just finished dinner and sat on the back porch, watching the sun go down. Mrs. Starbird asked, "How's school going?" and served us tea. We answered her pleasantries with what we were learning. And I commented on the evening sky. Its streaks of blues, pinks, purples, and oranges.

Cassie's Aunt Salem marveled, "Like someone painting a picture, and the water spilled over, smearing the colors into one another."

Mrs. Starbird agreed, "It is beautiful. The stars especially." In the distance, I heard a wolf howling. The animals were all back in the barn, safe and sound. The stars *were* shining, like bright white dots on a velvet-black backdrop. Entering the ranch from the back, we smelled some fresh baked apple tarts and headed for the sitting room. That's where the party was. Cassie's Aunt Salem moved indoors and played the piano in the sitting room. The windows were open, letting the breeze drift through, and the music spilled out into the evening.

Everyone had gathered around, listening to Aunt Salem at the piano. It was jazzier and more festive. Cassie's mom served tarts and tea. Finding an empty seat by the fireplace, we both joined in singing with her younger siblings.

The sweet cinnamon apple tart was even more tasty than the type my Aunt Julia baked. Looking up on the wall, I noticed a new addition. There were several framed drawings. It was unusual, and I stood to study it closer.

"Ahhh, you like?" Mr. Starbird moved over to stand behind me. "Someone had drawn this and gifted it to our family. It's El Chimo's prison just outside Los Alamos. That was right after the Collapse."

I leaned in to read the legend at the bottom of this map. "What was the place before it became a prison?" I asked.

Mr. Starbird studied his map. He frowned. "That's a good question. I don't honestly know. It was in the middle of nowhere. So, I'm not sure what it was used for."

"You've been there?"

"Yes, Cassie's uncle visits often. Once he took me with him when we went on one of our trips to that part of the state. It was long-since empty and abandoned." He pointed to the drawing next to it. "There he is, my brother Clay." A dashing figure in uniform holding a cavalry saber. "He was an officer in the regional militia."

Cassie joined us, nudged me, and nodded towards the fields. I nodded back. We rose and stepped toward the back door. "We're just going to take an evening stroll," Cassie announced.

"Sure, honey," her mother replied absently as she worked away on her crocheting. "Be careful, Cassandra."

I followed Cassie down the steps and around the side of the house, giggling. Near the back porch, crickets came out to play, and a frog croaked off to the right.

Cassie told me, "Aunt Salem talks about the times from her mama's age when music just came out of the wall. You didn't need to move away from your friend's company or take any piano lessons." We both laughed at the idea of it. It sounded hilarious, music out of a wall.

The dirt path led us through a field. Wheat on one side and meters of corn on the other. We ran along the path to the end where the crops met trees. Through the woods, the sun was setting, and the skies were turning a cobalt blue. At the creek, we sat on some rocks. "She also tells me of trains that ran on electricity."

I added, "I'd heard that. Someone said they could go from ocean to ocean in a day and a half. Can you imagine?"

"As much as I can imagine traveling with a scout. What's it like? I never asked you that?" Cassie skipped a stone across the creek.

I didn't look at my friend, knowing all too well what she was hinting at.

"Before? When you, and Librarian Way—you know?"

"We did what we had to do." I nodded, wishing we could go back to talking about nonsensical things that we'd never know in our lifetimes.

But she wouldn't let up. "Were you scared?"

"Yes." We both looked up at the darkening night sky. I added, "How are we going to catch your Uncle Clay?"

Cassie looked thoughtful. "I have an idea. If Uncle Clay is using resources from this ranch, I know who can tell us. We can track him from that. But we'll have to stop in the kitchen first."

Cassie introduced me, "Henrietta, I want you to meet Mateo." The worker had dismounted to speak with us. "He's Papa's supervisor."

I gave a small head bob and reached out to shake Mateo's

hand. Rough and strong. "Mateo, I heard you hired out some workers in the last few weeks?"

"Yes, senorita," He waved over the nearby rolling hills. "Work's been slow. We want to keep our men employed."

"Where are the men now? Some at school may be looking for jobs to get work experience."

Now Mateo showed some concern. "San Luis. Is there a problem? Should we have asked there first?"

I had a thought. "San Luis? Wasn't that where the old base was? The one in the painting?"

"Ah!" Cassie stared at me, stunned. "Do you think?"

I struggled to remember. "Maybe rocket engines at the old base?"

"Yes," came out weakly as Cassie nodded.

"Mateo. Who was the person you hired out your men to?"

"Your father said it was all right." His face gained a thoughtful look. "Clay, your father's brother, he asked for the men."

"Ah!" exclaimed Cassie. "How many did you loan out?"

"Just five." He scratched at his shoulder as he responded. "Clay told me they'd only be needed for the week."

Cassie reached into her basket and pulled out four warm empanadas, for Mateo.

~~~

It as a short walk back to the drawing room.

I shifted closer to Cassie. "Seems like we're not going to catch your uncle here."

"I guess so." She nodded. "Should we leave?"

"Anyone want another tart?" Mrs. Starbird asked, met with several yeses. I was one of them, as I returned to my spot beside Cassie. I glanced back at the drawings a few times. Something nagged at me about how they connected to my search.

William said, "We've learned why they're headed into

space." I had rejoined him at the large library in the city. Cassie had returned to school to update the principal on our schedule. I would meet her at Starbird Ranch later.

I couldn't imagine how the librarians could have found such information. We hadn't gotten our hands on any of the scalawags, yet.

William pointed to an empty part of the bookshelf. "Just heard back from an inquiry we sent to Korea." He paused for a moment, appearing thoughtful. "One missing document is related to the dangerous materials launched into space by North Korea, as the Collapse was happening."

I was puzzled. "North Korea?"

"They sent variants of the original virus into space." Holding a finger pointing up, he continued, "In self-contained virus environments."

"B-b-but..." I sputtered, "would those still be viable? After almost a hundred years?"

"Our experts don't think so. But we can't risk it."

The story about the rocket project. Again, I thought, *the original virus had brought on the Collapse.* "A virus spread through gasoline and other petroleum products had killed billions and left civilization in tatters!"

"Dangerous times, dangerous times," William muttered.

A question repeated in my mind. What did these people plan to accomplish by sending some rocket off to retrieve a deadly virus? From the little I knew, this technology was ancient, it hardly seemed real. Could they really get something off the ground? That would be a very bad thing. Surely, no one wanted to see that. There were some things best left alone in our world. But I didn't say anything to William. Glancing at the librarian, I realized he was almost unrecognizable. Tired and overworked.

William sighed heavily. "People I know are going missing. Most likely at the hands of madmen." He shakes his head again. "Madmen. Thinking they could change the world. Going back to the old tech that caused the worst for all of us."

"Most people aren't interested in going backwards." No, no matter how I looked at it, I didn't understand where they were going with this rocket plan.

I walked with Librarian Way out into the daylight. Footsteps rushed towards us from behind. Someone covered my mouth and nose with a smelly cloth. Unwillingly, I inhaled and felt the world spin around me. Fight back, my brain shouted. I managed to flay my arms. But the last thing I felt was scratchy burlap over my head.

~~~

I woke up in a dark room. It was damp and cool. I blinked until my eyes adjusted to the dark shadows, and I realized I was alone. It was a small cell. Looking around, I was sitting on a small dirty cot; it felt grimy under my hands. It sounded like someone was snoring, and someone else was pacing. I staggered to my feet and checked the room I was in. The two walls opposite each other were solid, but there were bars on the one side and partial bars on the back. There were noises in the distance. Where the hell was this? Who did this?

What did they want with kidnapping Librarian Way? Well, he did possess some knowledge about scientists and the rockets. This was ridiculous. I felt outraged and defeated. How would I get out of this? My tummy rumbled. Cold, tired, and trapped in God only knows where. It was night? Day? Where was William? He could be anywhere.

Moments later, Cassie crept in. "Henrietta."

She called softly and waved frantically for me to come to her. We made our way out without running into any kidnappers.

"How'd you find me?" My heart raced after escaping that fix.

"One of Mateo's men," she got out breathlessly. "He had

left Uncle Clay's people and saw you get ambushed. He followed, then ran back to the ranch and told us."

I didn't see anyone around. "Did you bring help?"

"Mateo is sending to the library for armed guards to come for Librarian Way. I couldn't wait while *you* were a captive and came ahead."

"My gods! You're brave."

She smiled. "What do we do now?"

* * *

"Cassie," I whispered, "over there." I pointed to a guard near the doorway. I asked, "Is that someone you know?" We had made our way to another large building nearby. So, they had recruited help with this crazy space mission. It looked like a possible ranch hand.

Cassie examined him, "Yes. one of my father's men." She rose out of hiding. "Let's do this." and strode confidently toward our enemy.

Standing and following, I spoke sotto voce, "He will listen to you, right?" I was hoping we weren't about to have a gang of ruffians jump us.

"Jesus!" Cassie sounded like she was speaking to a long-lost friend. The guard eyed us like something he didn't want to see.

"Little Cassie." That tone didn't sound promising. "What are you doing here? With her!"

I refused to be offended. I put on a smile and hoped I wouldn't need to pull any of the weapons I carried. "I'm so glad to see you. Cassie's father wants you to return to the ranch." I didn't know what I was saying but figured I had to say something.

"Yes, Jesus, we've been looking all over for you." Jesus' face had gone to confusion. Better than suspicious. I edged around him as Cassie held his attention. "The family's organizing a party. Want your help. We are inviting all the neighbors…"

Inside, my eyes adjusted to the dimness. There! I spied a figure, immobile in a chair. William. Tied hands and feet. He showed me his teeth with a wide smile. Moving closer, I saw some bruises, but he appeared mostly intact. I pulled my small knife out.

"Let me untie you." I quickly cut his bonds loose. Bet he was glad I had it on me now. Principal Hernandez always put a red mark on my ledger when one was found on me.

"We were right; they want to get the old virus and use it as a weapon. We have to rescue Professor Alvarado." The librarian flexed his free limbs and groaned, extending his arm up high toward a shelf. Seeing his sword, I climbed like a monkey to reach it.

* * *

Librarian Way and I left Cassie to find her parents' workers and entered the big warehouse together.

Way thought to enter the big warehouse alone. But I followed. People filled this room. Unexpected, but at the same time not surprising. William had dispatched the guard at the door with little effort. Panels of dials and displays covered the walls. There were men and women crowding this place. In the center, a metal tube, something like a thin grain silo, extended from a hole in the floor into the air. Shiny and huge. I'd never seen a rocket ship before, but I knew what I was looking at. That's it!

"How are we going to handle this?" None in the room appeared armed or ready to fight.

"We simply walk across and enter."

I felt that there was more steel in this room, and I had ever seen in my life. I struggled to keep my eyes focused on the open doorway that was our target. My brain was racing.

People around us. Any one of them might try to stop us. A strange machine sat there in the center of the room. My mind went real lean thinking of it, meant to launch into space.

Walking up to it, we'd lose our surprise.

I whispered to William, "Someone's rushing in."

William went silent. Not wasting time on my warning about the obvious.

My eyes couldn't adjust to what I was seeing. The closest it resembled was an open mineshaft circling the—*silo*. We stepped onto the shakiest of metal walkways leading to the middle of the room. Looking down, I spied the steel tube extending down into the depths. Hundreds of feet below us darkened into what must be the bottom of this device. More people were down there; we could hear their shouts. I figured possibly fifty people. Pipes, ladders, and cables on all levels ran to the ship.

I froze, looking at William. His face showed serious concern.

"Danger stands before us." His words bore into me. He glanced back. "We should leave."

I closed my eyes for a second. Then I shook my head. "We've got to stop it." I continued to the ship.

The ramp across that hole felt like walking a plank. Reaching the door, in the middle of this flimsy, gantry-like bridge, to the towering metal cylinder, gave me vertigo.

Once we entered, a man stood waiting, holding a sword. Clay!

William advanced with his own weapon drawn. Strange to see these blades face each other in this sleek metal space. Steel clashed against steel, ducking and weaving; the two were out for blood. This wouldn't end well for someone.

William jabbed and netted air. Clay swung to cut William's head off but caught, as William anticipated that and ducked. With a loud clank, William rolled his sword and lifted Clay's, tugging it. It flung out of his control and fell to the floor with a clang, where it skidded aside.

William glared, then commanded, "You're done. Give it up!"

I studied Clay's eyes; even without his sword, he appeared about to lunge. But the capsule lurched. Like a rat shaken like a dog.

"Brace!" shouted Alvarado. He stared at some gauges on the wall in front of him. "We're going up!"

Alvarado sat in the nearest chair and strapped in. I was torn between helping Way or a chair for myself. I sat hard, keeping my eyes on the fighters. At that moment, a force hit my back like a sledgehammer.

A roar filled the air. Everything before my eyes blurred for a moment. A small crack came to my ears. What had they done? Seeing the two men sprawled on the floor, I feared Clay's neck had twisted in an unnatural direction.

William lay splayed out. Alive was anyone's guess, but the force pressed him down with a vengeance.

"Professor! What happened?" I shouted over a storm of sound.

"Clay launched us!" His hands turned some dials and flipped some switches. Which seemed futile. What could possibly change what we were doing? My fears confirmed, he shouted, "Can't cancel it. I'm working to modify our launch profile."

The librarian groaned, loud enough for both of them to hear. When I thought we'd die, being sent with such force into the air, the stupidest thought came to me, but I yelled out anyway, "Are we ending up in space?"

"Best I can do." he panted and with effort, turned his head to look my way. "We've lost our trajectory but at least I've pointed us to land off the coast. Near California."

A familiar sound came from somewhere over my head. Was it? Yes, Moonlight Sonata, coming from a wall.

HOW IT ALL STARTED
OR THE SHORT HISTORY OF DOGS
HOWARD LORING

The young upright man, in reality still only a boy, had smelled the cooking meat from quite a distance. It was compelling. The wafting aroma mesmerizing, faint at first, but unmistakable, growing only stronger with each tentative step that he took, tearing at his empty stomach, forcing him ever forward.

Finding himself in unfamiliar territory, the youngster was understandably leery but also being very hungry, he continued through the thick underbrush with a determined purpose, in an unending quest. He knew he had to find nourishment, or he'd die. Then who would tell his strange story?

He'd eaten little the day before, too agitated by the gathering to come, for it was the first such endeavor he'd ever been permitted to accompany. ,Due to his age, before this, his never-ending chores of toting water from the river, or dragging tree limbs for the ever-present fire, had always been in proximity to his clan's current, well-defended enclosure. No excitement there, to be sure.

Of course, the youth had often longed to join in one of these gatherings, seemingly a hopeless wish, given his tender years. Still, he dreamed of the day for it was his undeniable path, as it was for each of the clan's boys. His time would come.

Then, on one of his last wood-collecting expeditions, he'd found a heavy branch that made for him, with little augmentation, a fine club. All of the mature, upright men had admired this new weapon, hefting and swinging it, testing its strength and balance. Each had been impressed by the unexpected discovery.

His uncle, headman of the clan, was most pleased, taking the find as an omen predicting a plentiful gathering. As a consequence, he allowed his nephew to join the upcoming venture. Sadly, this snap assessment had proved a mistake.

All gatherings were, and always had been, unpredictable things, the outcomes ever in doubt. Still, the clan's most recent encampment was extremely bountiful and of late all such expeditions had indeed been successful. Each time, the upright men had returned from them both cheerful and fully laden with meat.

The gathering party took to the great river before dawn, paralleling its meandering path, following the clan's standard operating procedure. Several times along the way, the uprights noticed promising footprints of the four legs at the water's edge, an event that engendered much excited interest. However, nothing came of them as they petered out once the ground became firmer inland from the river's bank, and so the determined party had returned each time to its previous route.

Gathering from the four legs was the best possible scenario for they could be beaten off their kill with little trouble. Often these kills were large animals. The four legs were formidable, always hunting in numbers that employed coordinated attack, and this strategy was highly effective in bringing almost anything down.

Yet, if they were attacked with sufficient preparation, successfully employing the tactics of surprise and overwhelming forces, the four legs would quickly relent and run off. The gathering party would then divide their efforts. Some would butcher while the others stood guard, encircling the kill, protecting the periphery of the grisly action.

The four legs always took a dim view of this, of course. They never retreated very far at first but hung at a distance, growling and snapping at each other in their displeasure over losing their kill. At some point though, compelled by hunger, they would be off in search of more game and often, this occurred before the meaty prize had been hacked into smaller pieces suitable for transport.

Other hunters in the area, such as the deadly long claws, were not so obliging. They were to be avoided at all times, for backing down and running away wasn't in their fierce nature. No, they attacked to protect their kill, and being much larger, they were highly aggressive and so more dangerous than the four legs.

Fortunately, their deeply resonate growl and loud, piercing cries could be heard at great distance and usually the ferocious creatures could be given a wide berth. Of course, this wasn't always possible, and chance meetings sometimes occurred. When they did, the standard outcome never favored the upright men.

The long claws had very long teeth, too.

The clan's ancestors had learned all these hard-earned lessons well, ages ago in the olden times. They hadn't been forgotten in the great interim since. Many well-known and oft repeated stories told of such horrifying encounters.

No, the four legs were clearly the best choice, and the clan always preferred gathering from them, but where were they now?

Late in the day and far from home, the weary upright men turned a sharp bend in the river only to find there a large horned one lying dead on the bank. Nothing seemed to be near it, although it was evident that the fresh carcass had been fed upon. The group advanced with alacrity to investigate, but only when they were up on the beast did the shocking truth become known.

Behind it, shielded by its very size, rested two sleeping cubs of the terrifying great one of the forest. This was a most surprising turn, having frightening consequences, for before the upright men could react, the cubs' mother broke from the nearby scrub. Very large and bristling, she was already snarling in anger at this intrusion, berserk now in her attempt to protect her young ones.

The startled group of gatherers were no match for her great bulk and massive claws. Several of them were immediately mauled before they could move away, and more were quickly run down and dispatched as her cubs, awakened by the unknown sounds, crying loudly in fear. This event propelled their mother into a true frenzy, and she lashed out viciously, unhindered, fueled only by her terrible rage.

The young upright boy, proudly clutching his fine new club, had been among the first gatherers to reach the dead horned one. Soon, he was caught with a tremendous, back-handed blow from the giant, swinging paw of the great one of the forest, who was madly thrashing about consumed by her impassioned slaughtering. It was as if a tree had hit him, and he was thrown unceremoniously into the great river.

This alone had saved him.

Of course, the youth couldn't swim, none of the upright men could. The always churning and never-ending river was very much viewed as a mystical thing by the clan, and so they had yet to even learn how to fish. But the boy, stunned, had nevertheless somehow floated up against a passing log that bore him downstream, and thus away from the horrid carnage still viciously transpiring on the now overly bloodied and gory bank.

After some time of desperately clutching about the log, he was rudely deposited ashore after his transport was beached having traversed a long bend in the river. The exhausted youngster had pulled himself further up on the bank and collapsed in a heap. Then, he smelled the cooking meat in the distance.

Naturally, the boy was unsure of his location, but that didn't matter. He had to eat soon, or he would never live to find his way home, if that were even possible now. He homed in on the enticing scent of roasting flesh.

Evening was near and approaching swiftly. Soon, he wouldn't be able to discern anything in the quickly growing gloom. However, he next saw the piercing light of a fire in the distance, shrouded by the surrounding forest.

The calling aroma, stronger now, turned his empty stomach into knots. He crept closer, taking care to move as quietly as he could, always forward towards the illumination, which at this point was enveloped by the deepening darkness.

At last, he could see the entire scene through the underbrush. A fine campsite had been laid in a small clearing rimmed by huge boulders. A giant fire, blazing away, cast flickering shadows against the rocks and shrubbery around them.

He saw no one about. It seemed the whole area was deserted, but for the meat, sizzling on a spit very near the fire, a huge hunk dripping tasty fat.

Who would leave such a treasure unattended?

Instinctively, he reached for his sharpened butchering stone, a most valued object that everyone carried during a gathering, a highly prized implement carefully chiseled with precision to fit the owner's hand. He found it missing as was, of course, his fine new club. He should have realized that the unforgiving waterway had already swallowed both of his precious tools.

The young upright man next judged himself not only lost and alone, which he was, but now totally weaponless as well.

Yet here he was wrong.

His finest instrument, possessed by every member of his

clan as well as those scattered about like them, had been minutely honed through time itself, from the very beginnings of his kind. It was a natural development unique to the now fully defined species, and no other living thing possessed it. Nothing came close, not even the lumbering, flat-headed men in the area who were generally so similar in other ways to the uprights.

This singular, superior weapon, at present being furiously employed to assess the situation, was his very large human brain.

This particular circumstance, however, was difficult to understand. Where was the owner of the meat, he wondered. And why had they left such an item unprotected?

Upright men cooked their food, of course, but they weren't the only ones to do so. The flatheads had fire as well, they, according to the clan's ancient lore, were the ones who'd first unlocked its hidden secrets. And they could be fearsome.

At last, he could stand it no longer. He broke through the brush and dashed to the spit, thinking only at first of grabbing the roasting meat and beating a hasty retreat. Yet, after laying hands on the greasy haunch, he instead had a much better idea.

The boy sank to his knees and bit into the still-sizzling flesh. Nothing had ever tasted so good to him, and he moaned in delight as the succulent juices dripped down his chin. Despite his earlier trepidation, he sat by the fire and ate with gusto, unconcerned now with what might happen next.

After savoring several mouthfuls, he reconsidered, thinking again of dashing off with his purloined meal, but he didn't. He was so exhausted he found that he couldn't move, only concentrate on the task at hand. He reasoned if the meat's owner did return and killed him, well at least by then, he'd die with a full stomach.

While munching away, he heard movement in the brush, the sound of someone approaching. The youngster, still chewing as fast as he could, sat in place and awaited his fate. At this stage, no other viable option was left open to him.

An upright man then appeared, but unlike any that he'd ever seen before. He was very tall, as tall as a flathead, but unlike them, he was thin and dressed in a bizarre fashion. He wore no stitched animal skins but some kind of covering that aside from his hands and face, totally wrapped him, clinging tightly to his body.

"Welcome," he said, but the boy didn't respond.

The newcomer then held out his arms, his palms open and pointed toward the youngster, who had stopped his mastication at the action. After a few seconds, the strange upright man dropped his hands. Then he smiled.

"Welcome," he said again, and this time, the interloper replied.

"I'm hungry," the young boy stated, as if that would explain everything. It did. The upright man smiled again and then sat on a large stone at the edge of the firelight.

"I know," he answered. "I cooked it for you. I knew you'd make your way here, to this clearing, tonight."

The boy's eyes opened widely as he considered this. Could it be so? Then with a shrug, he commenced his meal, knowing now that no immediate danger awaited him.

Yet, after swallowing his latest mouthful, he asked, "How?"

Now, the sitting man considered. He rearranged himself and, crossing his long legs, he leaned forward. After a bit, he answered.

"I know much," he stated as a fact. "I know that today was your first gathering, and I know the result. This adventure will make for you a fine story to tell."

At this, the boy only grunted. How would he ever get back to his clan, and how would he tell his story if he didn't? He knew not. Again, he sank his teeth into the roast but without frenzy now, in a slower and more deliberate pace, still thinking.

The stranger spoke no more, for the present only waiting for the boy to finish his meal. He understood that the youngster's mind was racing, trying to comprehend. He was content to sit and let him try.

Soon enough, the upright boy was satiated, his stomach now overly full. Still chewing his last bite, he stared down at the meat in his hands. Then he held it out to the stranger, offering the leftovers, but the man shook his head, declining.

"Take it with you," he said. "Just head back to the river and follow its bank but moving against the current this time. You'll be home by nightfall."

The boy nodded. Yes. It made sense. He would do so.

Then he thought of something else.

"What of the others?" he asked. Of course, this was a question about the ambushed gathering party. Here the man, while giving no answer, answered all with his silence.

The boy sighed, already knowing the truth. He'd reflected on the horrific episode while clinging to the log in the river. The great one of the forest was the most fearsome thing known, and the females were ever tenacious when their cubs were involved.

He thought first of his uncle, and then the others, the best uprights in his clan, each gone. Who would gather now? How would they ever survive this horrible loss?

The strange man understood his concerns. He felt sorry for the boy, but only in a peripheral, disconnected fashion. He had to remain above the fray, so to speak.

After all, time does march on, and always it will have its due.

"Other clans may welcome you," he said, in a comforting tone. "Your women and children are a wonderful gift to offer, and greater numbers help ensure the future. You must lead them, your clan, to another clan, and so save them."

The young upright was rendered speechless by this bold suggestion. How could he lead them, or what was left of them? He was just a boy, lost and helpless.

"You now have a powerful story," instructed the man, "for there's a grander purpose behind it. It has meaning beyond the tragedy itself, a lesson to be learned. So, they will listen and agree with your choices, why wouldn't they?"

"What purpose?" asked the incredulous youth, who certainly saw none. The whole thing was senseless as far as he could judge, the gathering nothing but a colossal failure. He boldly looked the man in the face, awaiting an answer.

"You must change the way you gather meat," the stranger said calmly, as if it were only natural to com thi[EaSS1] this new thought. "Another way must be found. A better way."

A moment went by, the boy deep in thought. "How?" he asked for a second time.

The strange man then slowly stood and, after holding out his hands in reassurance, he stepped over and sat closer to the boy.

"Why do you always chase the four legs away?" he quietly asked. "They are the ones who find your meat, after all. Do you not have to go out and waste your time tracking them all over again when the next gathering is needed?"

Now the youngster was really confused. How could you *not* chase them away? The hard-earned carcass was their prize, and they didn't give it up freely, without some sort of fight.

He began to answer as such, but the man cut him off by continuing, "Why not instead share a bit of the kill? It's easily done for they never run far, and you know this to be true. You could just throw them some of the meat."

"Why?" blurted the boy. "It's our food then. Why give it away?"

Again, the stranger smiled, understanding the boy's perplexed state. Change once made could take hold quickly, but embracing this choice often required great amounts of time to accomplish. Yet, small steps were still forward progress.

"But if you gave them some, they would stick close by," he explained, "and they'd gladly follow you home if you fed them along the way. Then you wouldn't have to find them when the meat was gone. Once you stop feeding them, they'd just go off in search of more, yet you could then follow them, is this not so?"

"But they are killers," said the boy, now the one trying to explain. How, he marveled, could such an absurd thing even be contemplated? This wasn't the established way.

"But do they kill?" asked the man, "After they're chased off? Do they attack you as you butcher the carcass, as the long claws would? No, they just get angry and then move on."

The boy shook his head. This was too much. It was unheard of. "That's never done," he stated flatly, as if it closed the subject.

Again, the stranger paused. Another approach was needed now, that much was evident. He'd held one in reserve, of course.

He leaned in some and quietly asked, "How did the upright men first come by fire, I wonder. There was a distant age, long ago when you had none, is this not true? Many stories from the olden times say as much, do they not?"

The boy had to admit that this was so. Everyone knew that the uprights had stolen fire from the flatheads, for they were the only ones who knew how to make it. As such, keeping the fire lit was always a prime concern for the clan.

Sometimes, it did go out, of course, a big problem. Other clans had to share then, but they only did so after some price had been paid. Finding fire in the forest was always possible. It had happened before, but it wasn't very likely, and the wiser course was to make sure that it never died in the first place.

But the boy, young as he was, had made this vital connection. Things change. Even the oldest of established ways must have been new once, he saw.

Yes, now he understood that change was very real, and perhaps inevitable. The day's bizarre events had proved as much. And he certainly didn't wish to repeat that particular change if he could help it, not if it could be avoided.

So, he mused after reflection, "Perhaps this would be better."

Then the young boy causally made another, most crucial connection. It was one that went beyond the moment at hand, critical as it turned out, to the very future of his entire species. And this simple train of thought would soon beget profound historic ramifications, for the conception easily defined by example the most important, pertinent tenant of humanity itself.

"Well," he said at last, "I guess I'll never know unless I try."

It turned out that he did try, and he succeeded, too. Once his devastated clan had effectively joined with another, the novel procedure was started, and it proved most advantageous. The four legs indeed followed the gathering uprights home, and they hung close by until the meat was gone.

Gatherings then became hugely rewarding. After the clan took to the forest, almost at once, the four legs would find a scent and, with little trouble, they would then run some prey aground. Abundant meat was thus found every day. There were also other benefits to the new arrangement.

The four legs were wonderful sentries. Nothing in the night could creep up on them or, by extension, the clan. They still kept their distance, but the animals inherently understood the advantages too, and so protected them.

They stayed. Living near the upright men supplied a safe environment in which to raise their young. True, their kill was taken from them, but the meat they were always given was enough, and this was their main concern.

There were only five of them at first, a small pack consisting of an alpha couple and three juveniles, two males and one female. Soon enough, more pups followed. This event was viewed as a good omen by the clan, and it was.

Then, after several seasons had passed, the four legs one night raised a cry in the dark. The hair-raising shrieks of the long claws were soon heard in the distance. A loud altercation then ensued, very brief but brutal, then all was quiet.

The next morning, the boy, who was now a strapping teenager, found at some distance a dead four legs, lacerated by the long claws. Her pack was nowhere to be seen, having run off in angry pursuit to harass the retreating perpetrator. The boy was unconcerned by this as they often ran off, and he knew from experience that they would soon return, demanding more meat.

Then he discovered the pups, newly orphaned and whimpering in the grass. They were young, hardly weaned, and almost without thinking, he took them inside the clan's fortified enclosure. They quickly became well-known.

Again, they were five, four brothers and a sister. They snapped and growled much, but due to their tiny size, they posed no real problems. That soon changed.

The two largest males, angling for dominance, became a danger because they consistently wished to demonstrate their fierceness. Within weeks, the boy, again without a thought, clubbed them both. That left two males and the female.

These pups grew and in time, joined the pack outside the upright's base. While not really tame, at a distance, they interacted much more with the clan and were even permitted entry into their enclosure if they wished. They were easily tolerated there, if not provoked by being approached too closely or quickly.

Once the young female bore pups, being proud, she brought them in for inspection, and they became well-known, too.

Again, the boy, now a man in earnest, clubbed the most vicious pups, and the offspring of the tamer survivors were more tolerant still. This now-entrenched protocol continued unabated. By the fifth generation, taking less than ten full seasons, the newest born pups, while hunting every day in the forest, stayed every night within the enclosure, content if still irascible at times.

The boy, a fully mature man now, realized they now preferred the company of the uprights to their wilder kin, still ensconced at the encampment's edge.

Ten more seasons came and went. The boy, having lived nearly thirty years, was now an old man. He had many good dogs by then, and they all loved him.

One day, he sat on the great river's broad bank. The scene was idyllic, shaded with the air neither hot nor cold, but he was thinking of another instance along the water's edge. That particular time, he recalled, had not been so pleasant.

He was remembering the day it had all started.

Then he heard someone approaching and the strange, upright man appeared, stepping from the brush. He looked exactly the same, as if the passing seasons had no hold on him. They didn't, of course, for he was a time traveler.

"Well, my friend," the man said to the one who was once only a lost and hungry boy, "you have done much good work. I knew you would. Does it please you?"

The old one, pausing to consider, reached over and scratched the ear of his nearest companion, which wagged its tail in response to the tender action. Then the upright realized that none of his dogs, before ever vigilant, had reacted in the least to the stranger's advance. Yet upon short reflection, the upright man knew this wasn't a surprising circumstance.

"I am content," he announced at last, "for the clan has much meat. And I'm amazed that the dogs now love and protect us. So yes, I'm pleased that your change was made, and that it was you who found me in the forest so long ago."

This sentiment caused the time traveler to laugh aloud. He sat near to the upright, as he had done the last time. Then he caressed the dog stretched prone between them.

Again, the animal wagged its tail, thumping slowly this time.

"But you were the one who found me," the tall man pointed out. "You could have given up in the river, or at its bank. Yet you didn't; you bravely pushed on."

The old man hunched his shoulders, replying, "I was hungry." They both enjoyed this banter, each chuckling some. After a time, the old man asked, "What will happen now?"

"More change," was the time traveler's answer. "It is always so. It will always be so, forever."

The old man nodded, knowing it was true.

"But how?" he probed, wishing clarification. "What new changes come? What will happen next?"

The stranger leaned in, again as he had done at their last encounter, and after a bit, he answered with, "The upright man is a strong animal, and he thinks. Now he can hunt, not just gather. So, he can provide for and protect himself well."

The old one nodded.

"But when an upright man takes himself a family," came next, "he will always protect them, too."

The old one nodded again, adding, "Yes."

"The families of his kin are also his family," the stranger next explained, "for they are related, and when many such families join, they become a clan, as yours did. Each member of this clan is now also his kin, for they are all connected in some way. So, a man will protect his clan as well as his own, for they are the same."

"Yes," the old one said once more.

"Now," the man said, "you have dogs in your family, and they will protect you too, for they are a true part of your clan, as well. Because of them, your clan will become much stronger.

Other clans will do this also, and then all clans will grow stronger."

"I see it." The old one nodded, but next, he saw something else. It was another correlation. He didn't like its portent, but still he understood well enough.

"They will squabble with each other for the best meat," he predicted. "Fight over the finer ground that has it. And soon, they will club each other over it, to provide for, and so protect *their* family."

"Yes," the stranger concurred, but then he added, "Yet, at some point, certain clans will join together, forming a tribe, and things become very different then."

The upright man was surprised by this. "These new tribes, they will not fight each other?" he asked.

"No, they will fight," was the answer, "That's not my meaning. I mean that tribes fight for a different reason, a new reason. Tribe members will do battle for those not related to them, for in tribes, there are many who aren't connected by family ties."

This new concept once more took the old one aback. Who would fight for those who weren't related? Then he thought of his beloved dogs, so different from the upright men, and he understood, again making the leaps in thought.

Next, once seeing the consequences, the old man expanded upon them. Yes, he easily sensed the broader leaps involved. His very large brain worked very well.

"Such new tribes, after growing ever stronger, will then band together?" he asked of the stranger.

"In the far future, yes," was the answer. "Tribes become states, and states become mighty nations. The strongest of these nations will grow further still, becoming vast empires."

The old man was amazed by this declaration. It was a great vision, no doubting that. He felt humbled.

The stranger stood slowly and added, "All because of the dogs, my friend. It will happen because you made this vital connection and took them in. Everything now changes because you tried something different by thinking in a new and untested way."

The astounded upright sighed after this. He turned to look at the time traveler before him. Again, he hunched his shoulders, adding a wistful smile.

"I was hungry," he reiterated, as if that explained everything.

It did, and the tall stranger then walked away for the last time.

COCOON

SCOTT CIRAKOVIC

Scott Cirakovic is a fantasy and science fiction author from Australia. He currently lives in New South Wales with his wife, two children, three dogs, cat, rabbit, and two birds in what he describes as "the zoo."

He has graduated from James Cook University with a Bachelor of Business and has served in the Australian Army as a commissioned officer for over ten years. Scott grew up in country Victoria in a small town called Korumburra, where his parents owned the local video and convenience store, which helped kickstart his love of the fantasy and science fiction genres in all their forms. He has lived all over Australia's east coast and travelled internationally extensively.

To follow Scott's writing journey, sign up for his newsletter at scottcirakovic.com or follow him on social media.

Harry hit the ground hard, sending a cloud of dust up around him. With practiced precision, his knees bent to take the shock. His exoskeleton enhancements helped transfer the force through his body, so his legs didn't break from the two-story drop. Within half a second, he was moving again, heading for the burnt-out car not far from the overpass he had just jumped off, his enhanced legs working overtime to get him moving at almost twenty kilometres an hour.

A quick burst of power sent him flying over the car, although a split second too late as he felt a round bounce off the back plate of his armour while he was in the air.

"These raiders are getting better," he said absently to himself, checking the small tablet on his right wrist bracer which displayed his vital signs. "Slightly elevated heart rate and adrenalin, no haemorrhaging," he said, ignoring the rounds bouncing off the car and ground around him.

Quickly raising his head, Harry counted no less than seven of the raiders, all dressed in old leathers and tattered clothing, firing wildly with rusted out hunting rifles. He was surprised they had so many weapons and even more surprised they were wasting ammunition so quickly. The old hunting rifles that farmers used in the old days were hard to come by, and ammunition was a precious commodity regardless of weapon type.

The raiders currently had the high ground on the overpass and seemed uninclined to leave it while they still had ammunition. Checking the small tablet on his left bracer this time, it became apparent that Harry had allowed himself to be trapped in a firing lane. It showed a 3D map of the surrounding area, generated by a combination of recovered Google Maps data that had survived the great data compromise of 2075 (thought to be the work of Kim Jong-Song, 5th Supreme Leader of North Korea), and a small sonar pulse emitted every ten seconds.

The map showed that he was stuck on the Old Northern Road with large concrete walls on either side. Even with his exoskeleton legs, Harry couldn't jump over the old noise barriers which were amazingly still standing, and despite the lightweight composite armour, protecting his vitals, he knew he couldn't charge the raiders without significant injury.

"I should have known this was a trap," he reprimanded himself. "This is why I never bloody liked Brisbane."

A few quick taps on his map tablet were all he needed to unleash the last combat drone from the belt of his exoskeleton legs. The drone was only the size and weight of a book, one of the old paper ones that hadn't been around for years, other than in museums. It packed one hell of a punch for its size, armed with a twenty-round magazine of 9mm ammunition and high explosive laced into its body. Following the commands Harry had entered on his tablet, the drone quickly flew up to the overpass. With a quick burst from its 9mm cannon, he dispatched four of the seven bandits who had stood in the open, trying to figure out what the drone was.

"Not too bright," Harry muttered, using the distraction to sprint away from the overpass and the remaining bandits. His enhanced legs carried him quickly out of range, although it was probably unnecessary as he heard a loud explosion, followed by the screams of the remaining raiders as the drone self-destructed near them.

Despite having almost thirty kilograms of additional weight strapped to his body in armour, weapons, and ammunition, Harry made very quick time. He still needed to cover fifty kilometres of ground through the urban terrain of what used to be northern Brisbane. At a top speed of twenty kilometres per hour and enough stimulant injections to keep his energy up, he figured he could easily make it in under three hours. But his endorphin level quickly came to a crashing low, his right vitals bracer flashing with the sudden change.

"You know this isn't an approved program for a second-class cadet, Mr Branning," a loud, bodiless voice echoed from nowhere.

"I know, sir," Harry replied, not slowing his pace.

"Well, let's see how you handle this then," the voice said ominously.

Within seconds, Harry could hear the roar of approaching beaten-up, motley painted technical vehicles. The sound of heavy metal music and the hollering of more bandits adding to the cacophony of noise coming towards him. A quick pulse of his map bracer showed a corner store with a veranda out front only a couple hundred metres ahead of him, which could give him some high ground to fight from. Renewing his efforts, he pushed himself and his exoskeleton legs to the limits, the roar of the approaching bandits urging him on as they saw him and sped up for the kill.

Normally, he would have used one of his drones to slow down the vehicles and gain some time to get into a better tactical position, but he had used his last drone at the overpass, meaning his only chance was to reach the building before being run down. The roar of the technical engines was deafening by the time he attempted just that. Flexing his enhanced legs and leaping with all his energy towards the veranda, confident that it would provide a good enough firing position to destroy the bandits' vehicle.

Pain lanced through his entire body as the sky and ground became one big blur of colour, wind streaming past his ears until he hit the ground with a hard crack. The Ute had caught him and hit his legs as he jumped, sending him spinning through the air and landing in the middle of the road; his right bracer was squawking an alarm with all the injuries he suffered from the impact and fall. Harry didn't even have a chance to look for his rifle before the roar of the engine brought his attention back to the situation.

The old beaten-up Ute completed a hard handbrake U-turn and barrelled back down the road towards him, significantly faster than Harry could move with a destroyed exoskeleton and multiple fractures in his legs.

Right before the Ute hit, the world froze, crumbling in a

shower of thousands upon thousands of pixels, the simulated pain in his body instantly easing as his consciousness slipped back into his real body. Swearing softly to himself, he flexed his muscles gently and prepared himself for what was about to happen as the virtual reality cocoon slowly shut down and released his body back into the real world.

As the cocoon tilted back to a vertical position, the doors opened outwards to show exactly what Harry knew was waiting for him. His tactics instructor, Captain Channing.

"Noting your poor performance on the last TEWT, Mr Branning," Channing said, holding his command tablet behind his back, dress uniform crisp, and displaying an impressive number of medals. "I expected you to be practicing your conventional combat team manoeuvres." Harry sighed quietly as he stepped out of the cocoon and stood to attention. He had never been able to master the control needed to be good at the tactical exercise without troops program which simulated a lieutenant in control of an infantry combat team during conventional operations.

He still couldn't believe that lieutenants used to only command a platoon in combat, and they had to be directly in the fight to do it, often shouting commands over the din of battle. Controlling a combat team using a command tablet from a command post kilometres away was hard enough, but that was what was expected of him if he wanted to graduate.

"The Australian government does not pay you to play games," Captain Channing continued. "If you want to graduate from the Royal Military College as a lieutenant, you will need to drastically improve your skill at commanding soldiers in combat. Your fixation on running the escape and evade scenarios will not help you do that. Do you understand, Mr Branning?"

"Yes, sir," Harry answered dutifully, still standing at attention.

"But considering you did run the program, let's see how you did."

Harry sighed again, this time almost loud enough for Captain Channing to hear. Captain Channing was one of the most decorated combat officers instructing at the Royal Military College - Duntroon, having fought in North Korea in 2119, the island of Tingpin, once known as Taiwan, in 2121, and in 2125, Burma, which had changed names between Burma and Myanmar at least four times in the last hundred years.

Apparently, he had been promoted several times but kept getting himself demoted so that he could stay near the front lines, commanding combat teams and battle groups. "You made it quite far all things considered, though you made several tactical mistakes. You sacrificed your android dog in an urban engagement which you could have bypassed, wasted several drones on individual targets as you moved through the city, and in that final engagement, you surrendered the high ground of the overpass, meaning you needed to rely on your final drone when you could have easily dispatched the raiders with your kinetic rifle, had you stood your ground in the first instance. Overall, barely a passing grade."

"Yes, sir," Harry said again, knowing any protests about his performance would be futile.

"I understand the attraction of running these simulations, Mr Branning. They perfectly replicate our combat abilities and technologies but allow us to fight in alternate scenarios, which is why the video game industry is one of the Australian Defence Force's biggest recruiting pool. But you need to focus on your tactics more if you ever want to be more than a passing grade officer."

"I understand, sir."

Without saying anything further, Captain Channing left the room, leaving Harry standing among the thirty empty VR cocoons. This room had once been a lecture hall where over two hundred cadets would sit and receive lessons from the instructors, all of whom were required to be posted to RMC strangely enough. Harry never understood the logic behind this. How could they provide contemporary instruction if they weren't in a combat unit doing the job?

He was glad those days were over. Now, they only had one full-time instructor per class. Their lessons on tactics, leadership, ethics, and all the other subjects they were required to study were done virtually, through the cocoons. Officers assigned to give lessons could do so from any unit across the country or even while deployed in an active combat zone, based on their recent expertise. They could create any virtual world they needed to deliver the lesson, which were often recreations of battles they had themselves fought in. He also couldn't imagine being in a class of hundreds.

History was by no means his area of expertise, but he didn't understand why the Army of the past had needed so many officers, his own class being only thirty-one people. He guessed it was because in the old days, they expected officers to take care of soldiers, instead of just leaving that to the senior non-commissioned officer, allowing them to focus on tactics and command of the battle space—something that had made the Australian Army significantly more efficient in combat.

Harry looked at the digital leaderboard that hung in every room at RMC and showed the current standing of every cadet based on their performance. He currently sat twenty-sixth out of thirty-one cadets. Sighing loudly now that Captain Channing had left, he climbed back into his VR cocoon and fired up one of the training TEWT programs, determined to improve his standing and prove to everyone that he could command a combat team effectively. The soft gel-like pads nestled into him comfortably as he closed his eyes.

The cocoon tilted rearwards as the doors closed over Harry, starting to hum gently as his consciousness was pulled into the virtual world he'd selected. He found himself in a familiar armoured command post vehicle, his command tablet in his hand and rifle slung behind his armour. He was sitting in an uncomfortable bucket seat which wasn't designed for legs in exoskeletons, the small earwig in his ears which both protected his hearing and provided access to the subspace communication voice nets (SCVNs in Army language) pressing against his helmet.

It was sweltering in the command vehicle, and he knew it would be the same outside where his combat team was currently assembled, awaiting his orders. Ninety men in full combat suits, all linked to his command tablet and armed with the most devastating modern weapons, all ready to kill and destroy anything in their path to fulfill his commands.

Looking at the command tablet, Harry saw the familiar tactical overlay describing his mission for this TEWT—a blocking task in the liberation of the capital city of Burma in 2125. This TEWT had been programmed by Captain Channing and was based on the mission in which he earned his Victorian Cross, and the one where his entire combat team except for five men were killed. It was by far the most challenging TEWT in the system.

Knowing he only had an hour before regular classes began, and he would have to either abandon or save the program's status for later, something which always annoyed Harry because he lost precious seconds when he returned, figuring out exactly what he was up to. Harry quickly formulated his plan and delivered orders to the waiting soldiers, sending them on their way to battle, almost ten kilometres away, while he monitored their progress on his tablet, sitting in the rear of the command vehicle.

The digital battle didn't take long. Within twenty minutes, Harry had lost a platoon, in a narrow street simply trying to get to the blocking position, to an ambush he hadn't anticipated. Once the remainder of his combat team arrived, they were set upon by the enemy almost instantly before they could erect any type of defensive structures, killing another half of a platoon, but at least they manage to fend them off.

Within forty minutes of commencing the mission, his blocking force had been surrounded, cut off from retreat, and was systematically being destroyed as he watched helplessly from his safe position in the armoured command vehicle. Sighing in disgust at himself and his poor performance, he cancelled the simulation, ending the battle prematurely rather than letting the destruction of his combat team drag out.

As the cocoon released him again, he noticed that most of his class was assembled in the room already, waiting for Captain Channing to come and tell them what they would be doing for the day. Not wanting to talk to any of them, he stayed silent beside his cocoon. For the first time in Harry's year at RMC, Captain Channing was late, which caused an avalanche of whispered conspiracies among the other cadets while they waited.

Almost thirty minutes passed like this, until finally, Captain Channing entered the room, yelling, "Stand fast!" bringing them all to attention.

"Rest, ladies and gentlemen," the commanding officer of RMC, Lieutenant Colonel Shrubby said, coming to a halt directly in front of them in his crisp uniform. "I am here to congratulate you all for graduating from the Royal Military College—Duntroon and to wish you all the best for your first posting. Captain Channing has all your first assignments and will hand out your new rank slides in short order. Remember, you have had the best training in the world and will soon be commanding the best soldiers in the world; ensure that you make us all proud."

Without anything further, Lieutenant Colonel Shrubby left the room, leaving thirty stunned cadets standing with their mouths open.

"What just happened, sir," one of the cadets finally asked

Captain Channing, who had started silently down the line, slipping lieutenant rank slides onto their uniforms.

"Australia just declared war," he answered softly. "You are all being commissioned early and sent to combat units. Your training is over; your education is about to begin."

UNDER A CRETACEOUS SUN

M. J. KONKEL

The pink sun rising behind Kat promised a wonderful day as she bounded down the wooden steps, humming a tune. Ahead, a young boy sat. "Hey, kid," she called out, "Make a little room please."

He craned his head around. "Sorry!" He scooted over. "Hey lady?"

"Lady?" Kat stopped and faced him. "Just how old do you think I am?"

The kid shrugged. "Older than me."

Kat chuckled. "Well, you got me there. Got a name?"

"I'm Tommy. Hope I didn't make you feel bad—for being old. You're not old like my mom, and you're real pretty for being a lady too."

Kat smiled. "What do you want, kid?"

"Do you know what kind of dino that is?"

Kat turned her gaze to where the kid pointed. A long, thin, serpent-like head stuck out of the river. "That's a pleo, Tommy. You only see them once the water starts to warm. There're a lot of dinosaurs out there to be worried about, but not these. They eat only fish."

"Really?" Tommy squinted. "It looks pretty scary."

"Take it from me, kid. I know a thing or two about this world. You just got here, but this is where I grew up."

"Cretacia," Tommy blurted out what everyone called this version of Earth. "It's not like the Earth where I used to live. I mean lots is the same, but we got no dinosaurs there."

"Did you know my mom and dad were among the original castaways before everyone was rescued?"

"Really? Tell me about them."

"Another time. I'm running late." Kat gave the boy a fist bump and bounded down the steps.

The boy was forgotten by the time she reached the docks. More important things on Kat's mind. Ahead, a quadcopter sat on a floating landing pad. A man waited there; two others already sat in the copter. Kat was the last to arrive and was late. She wondered if the last glass of wine was to blame. It had been a late night. Being honest with herself though, she was almost always the last to arrive everywhere. And being late had never bothered her before. Not the time to worry about it now.

"Hello. Katrina Faberley, I presume?" A man stood between her and the quadcopter. Kat recognized his voice from the two-minute call before her evening celebration. Her first impression upon seeing him was the man seemed smaller and, with his balding head, older than she had expected.

"Yeah. Everyone calls me Kat though. I'm… I'm sorry for holding you all up."

"No worries there. We've not been here long. I'm George DeMooney." He thrusted out his hand. "Been told you're the best guide money can buy here."

Kat chuckled as she took the hand. "Don't know who the heck told you that load of potatoes, but I know my way around well enough out there. Have to warn you, though, I've only guided hunters out into the bush 'til now. This guiding from up in the air thing is new to me."

DeMooney chuckled. "This should be like candy from a

baby for you then. Not that I'm a baby, mind you. Well, time doesn't wait. And neither does Anita. Take the front seat." He nodded toward the copter.

Kat thought he would have wanted the front seat for himself. She also had expected a lot more questions, but he was the boss for the day. As long as she got paid at the end of it... Heading toward the copter, she noticed cameras attached to its frame. Did he just record as she stammered her introduction like an idiot? She smiled and waved awkwardly at the camera.

The boxy clear plexiglass bubble of the cabin sat on a tubular frame. Four long booms jutted out at angles away from the frame, and a prop unit sat on the end of each boom.

Kat nodded at the pilot, Anita, and buckled her own safety straps into place, then plucked the helmet off the floorboard in front of her.

Anita nodded before returning her attention back to her instruments. Kat glanced at the controls, wondering what it would be like to be the pilot. Maybe someday.

She peered over her shoulder at Denard Robertson, the outdoor film star. An Australian bush hat covered his wavy, blond hair and clean-shaven fortyish face. Groomed for his role as an outdoor video star. "Hi." She nodded. The man's lips widened into a grin.

"Well... hello there."

Kat faced front at that, now sure the rumors were true. The man believed his smile was all it took with women.

Kat had a sense of being out of place, the baby of the group. Even the pilot must be in her thirties. With her freckles, thin build, and auburn pigtails, Kat felt the others must think of her as a kid even though she was now twenty-three and one day. More than once, her guided clients had asked her whether her father had signed off on her working as a guide. The last one ended up with a bleeding fat lip. The memory brought a frown. It had cost her a check and forced a couple of days of mooching off family.

Her armrests faintly vibrated as the engines purred to life. Then the four rotors spun up, and their humming drowned out the engines.

"Taking her up." Anita pushed forward on her left-hand control stick. The pitch of the engines increased, and the craft rose smoothly off the pad.

Kat tried to contain herself. Her first quadcopter ride. Told herself it was no big deal but knew the stupid grin on her face told the world otherwise.

She glanced sideways. The pilot was perfectly capable of giving an aerial tour, and Kat suddenly wondered why DeMooney had hired her to be the guide on the trip. Perhaps he thought having someone born here would lend more authenticity to the episode. No matter. It was a little extra cash during tight times for her.

"Which way, Miss Faberley?" DeMooney asked from behind Anita.

"Call me Kat, please."

"Sorry! Which way, Kat?"

"It's migration season. There'll be all kinds of dinosaurs heading north out on the prairies." She pointed east. "That way." The direction was obvious—Anita would have chosen the same.

She had seen enough other versions of Earth, including Prime, to know her world was special. Did everyone think where they grew up was special? The wide Mississippi fell away below. As they banked toward the still rising sun, cream-colored bluffs rose high over the valley before them. The copter narrowly cleared the top of a bluff, and Kat pointed out a few spooked dactyls taking flight off the edge of the bare limestone below. The aerodynamic creatures, with their long, thin bodies, even longer wings, and ridiculous beaks, caught an updraft and glided out above thin strands of mist suspended above the valley.

Their copter flew the other direction, passing over a seemingly endless number of small valleys turning green with spring. After a while, the landscape changed, becoming a vast prairie, covered with a mix of tall, brown and short, green grasses.

Kat spotted a herd of sauropods ahead. Super-sized bodies, ridiculously long necks, relatively small heads, and tails even longer than their necks. She rambled on about what she knew about them to DeMooney.

"Looks like Flintstones' dinos to me," Robertson said.

Kat chuckled. Not the first time she'd heard the comment. "Most people just call them brontos. The males are johnnies; the females are called jennies."

"Could we come around to the left a little more and get alongside them?" DeMooney asked Anita.

Anita brought them around. Behind her, DeMooney punched away at the pad in his hand, swiveling and zooming the cameras Kat had spotted earlier.

They soon left the brontos behind and gained altitude, turning southeast. Ahead, a new herd appeared. These were different. As their copter approached, a pentatops raised its huge head toward them. An enormous shield behind the head sported two long lance-like spikes, and a curved horn came off its nose.

"A lot of people I guide mistakenly think these are *Triceratops*," Kat said. "We call them pentas—five—because of the two additional big spikes coming off the edge of their shields."

Again, Anita kept the copter a safe distance away as DeMooney shot more footage.

"Take us down over there near that boulder." He pointed a finger over Anita's shoulder.

"Sorry." Anita shook her head. "This tour's air show only. Nothing was said about going down."

"I'll pay an extra two Clevelands if you take us down."

"Sorry. Too risky."

"Three," DeMooney said.

After a pause, Anita said, "Four thousand... and if either of you get hurt, I'm not liable."

"All right." DeMooney grinned. "Deal."

Kat understood Anita's reluctance. Pentas moved surprisingly fast. If DeMooney wanted to get closer to some unpredictable animals, the brontos would have been a safer choice. She opened her mouth but then closed it again. DeMooney was paying her good money to be their guide. Enough to not have to worry for the next week. They would just have to be careful.

As Anita set the copter down a few hundred yards away, the pentas dug up dirt with their front hoof-like claws. They lowered and shook their hoods as they quickly withdrew into a circle, horns pointing outward.

"Typical behavior when they feel threatened," Kat said.

As soon as they were down, DeMooney turned to her. "This is where you earn your pay." He and Robertson hopped out.

It dawned on Kat just as she hopped out of the copter behind them; DeMooney wanted video footage of Robertson approaching the dinosaurs as if it were bravery. Actually, it was foolishness—if anyone asked her. But they needed her to get them safely close to the animals, and they were paying her to know how close safe was. She shook her head at the thought. Safe was such a relative term when it came to dinosaurs. She caught up to the two and took the lead.

Then she stopped and crouched. "About as close as we should push it. Those bulls are already agitated."

"All right, sugar," Robertson said. "Out of the way now and let the man do his thing."

Kat scowled but slid behind them. DeMooney gave her a sympathetic smile and a little shrug before raising his camera. Robertson described the pentas, reminding his future audience just how dangerous his being there was.

"And those two horns on the shield are each at least three feet long and come to a wickedly sharp point. They use those for protection against the giant rexes that follow them around on the prairies here." He let his gaze sweep across the landscape as if he searched for rexes. Kat almost giggled but caught herself. DeMooney wouldn't be happy with that. She then bit her lip so as not to laugh when Robertson's head stopped swiveling to give the camera a profile of his face before he snapped it back toward the camera.

"Well, thankfully, there aren't any rexes around. Oh, I would hate to meet one of those out here. But could you imagine what would happen if one of these beasts behind me suddenly charged? With those spikes? I'd be skewered like a tomato ready for the barbeque."

Kat rolled her eyes. Robertson stared into the camera though, not at her. Why did people watch this buffoon? It had to be for the wildlife and scenery.

DeMooney lowered his camera, and they started back to the copter. Anita had left the rotors spinning. If needed, she was ready for a fast takeoff. Kat constantly peeked back over her shoulder to be sure the pentas hadn't begun to act crazy.

They reached the copter, and Robertson came up behind her. An unwelcome hand touched her elbow. She certainly didn't need any help. And then his other touched her buttocks.

She slapped it away. Her foot spun off the nerf step. Her right morphed into a fist. But then, she thought of the money she hadn't received yet. The hand opened, and both snapped to her hips instead, as she spun around, her teeth clenched.

"What's wrong, sugar? Tell me you didn't like that." A grin still on his face. It almost got him a knee between the legs.

"If you ever touch my bottom like that again," she yelled

over the hum of the rotors, "I'll put a bullet in yours." She glared straight up into his face as she suppressed an urge to bloody his nose. Still smirking, he winked. Her hand balled up into a fist again.

"Whatever!" Robertson turned away. A moment longer, and she would have wiped the look off his face. He climbed into the seat behind hers. Her teeth were still clenched. Dislike of him had turned to hatred. Didn't he realize she wasn't joking about the bullet?

She climbed into her seat and rammed the buckles into place. "Mr. Robertson, I meant what I said."

"Meant what?" DeMooney asked.

"Nothing," Robertson said. "Just a private little joke between us."

Try it again. We'll see if you think it's still funny. If she ever got a job like this again, she would demand full payment upfront. As Anita took them back up, Kat took a deep breath. She calmed herself as they flew south for a while.

"Those must be the rexes." DeMooney pointed to the left.

"Uh, yeah." Kat put Robertson out of her mind for the moment and focused on her job. "*Minneasarus rex*, similar to the extinct T-Rex in size and appearance, but with even bigger heads, and with spikes coming out of their backs."

Anita banked the copter. They circled around the animals several times. At one point, one of the rexes directed a loud bellowing roar at them. DeMooney giggled as he got it on film. No one even thought about landing near the monsters.

Again, they turned south. DeMooney commented on the beauty of the land. Kat smiled, knowing she sometimes took it for granted.

To her right, she spotted another small herd of brontos and alerted the others. Seemingly unconcerned about the copter, the animals lowered their heads down to the green carpet. Kat knew the grass was a couple of feet tall already; the animals' size made everything else seem smaller.

"This is it!" DeMooney pointed. "Take us down."

"Uh-uh. Four Cleves was for one trip down," Anita said. "It's freaking dangerous walking around down there. The animals will eat you, stomp you, spear you—"

"I'll add an extra Cleve to the offer."

Anita shook her head.

"Okay, fifteen hundred."

Anita sighed. "I'll take two. Not a buck less. That'll be six thousand extra you owe me when we're back."

"All right. But no more haggling over more money. If we want down, you take us. Deal?"

"Fine," Anita agreed. Her voice suggested she'd hoped for more, but Kat thought Anita couldn't be too unhappy about some extra cash.

"Ah, maybe going down isn't such a good idea right now." Kat pointed ahead. They could now see over the tall trees on the small hill beyond the brontos. The south side was covered with grass, and at the bottom, a rex seemed to be following the brontos. Probably their scent trail.

"Wow! That's a monster. New plan." Everything excited DeMooney as if he were a big kid. He fiddled with his camera feeds. "Buzz over its head. I gotta get footage of that beast roaring. Make sure we get close enough that it really reacts."

Kat had to trust Anita's judgement to keep them safe. Nevertheless, she gripped the armbars of her seat as the copter flew within fifty feet of the monster's head. It reared back and opened its enormous jaws. The roar drowned out even the rotors' hum as deep bass tones vibrated the whole copter.

Kat gazed down at the open maw and froze. The beast's tongue seemed as big as she was. Its teeth were pointy pylons. The cave-like throat could swallow her whole and not even choke.

"Man, that was impressive," DeMooney said. "Now do that again, but lower. Level with its head. I want a shot of it roaring out horizontally at us."

"Not too close," Kat warned Anita.

"Just close enough to get it to open its jaws again," DeMooney said. "I can zoom in on it."

Kat almost said something but then reminded herself she had to hold back her usually quick tongue. Getting on the wrong side of a rex was hardly a good idea, but she thought she had been doing pretty good so far, and she needed to continue acting professionally. The definition of professional, after all, was one who gets paid. Though something about this didn't feel right in her gut.

The tip of the rex's tail swung back and forth as they approached. Kat's stomach clenched. Anita flew the copter slowly past the animal's head but stayed a good thirty yards away. Kat glanced to her right. She knew of more than one incident where someone was nearly caught by a second dinosaur because of the focus on the first. There was no second rex though.

The beast roared in their direction and then stretched its head out. Took three giant strides toward them. But they had already buzzed a safe distance away by then. Kat loosened her grip on the armrest and took in a deep breath.

"Great footage!" DeMooney cheered. "Gotta get back to those brontos. Do a fly-by and get some type of reaction from them. At least, get them to lift their heads and look at the camera. Then we need to land somewhere. Get some more footage of Denard on the ground with them."

"These animals are dangerous," Kat said.

"Not my first rodeo, sugar. I've been around danger before," Robertson said.

"His fans want to see him, not just the animals," DeMooney continued. "And the more dangerous it appears, the better for our ratings."

Being called sugar chafed. If Robertson thought she was sweet, he'd find her more sour. She might have to find an opportunity to put one in his backside yet. Accidents happen, after all, right? Like after tripping over a rock? "I'm not saying we shouldn't go down. But we gotta be careful. All I'm saying."

"Like I said, it only needs to *appear* dangerous," DeMooney said.

Meanwhile, Anita guided the copter around for a last pass before heading to the brontos. She flew low again but gave the rex a wide berth.

With the rex behind them, they approached the hill, and the copter rose toward the tops of the trees covering it. Once they came over the crest, the enormous brontos became visible again off in the distance.

A large flock of pteradacts suddenly sprang from the tall oaks where they'd been roosting.

The pteradacts' flying was unlike birds which flew in flocks, even when spooked. The pteradacts went in all directions. Everywhere. The copter caught in their midst.

Only the copter's clear bubble was between them. One banged into the cabin's bubble next to her. She threw her hands up as another smacked against the front. The bubble cracked. Blood splattered to the right on the bubble. Still another smacked the front.

Then one crashed into the pilot's side.

The copter suddenly banked hard left, then right. Then left again.

Screams erupted from behind but barely registered to Kat. Anita's head slumped forward.

The copter dipped. Dropped. Kat didn't know how to fly the copter, but she had to do something.

Her hand shot out. Grabbed the stick on Anita's far side. She'd pushed the stick forward to go up. Kat pushed it the same direction. Hoped she was right.

Their descent slowed. The ground still came up fast though. Too fast.

Kat pushed harder on the stick. Already as far forward as it would go though. Their descent slowed, but they still dropped fast.

They hit. Hard. But not dead, Kat realized.

But the pilot-side rotor boom came down over a small boulder. It buckled upward.

The blade from the warped assembly caught the blade of the rotor behind it. Both blades disintegrated. Exploded.

An explosion rang inside the cab an instant later. A large carbon composite fragment of the copter blade had penetrated the cabin and now poked out of the dash. It had whizzed past within inches of her head.

She reached over Anita's body and hit the switches to kill the remaining two rotors before they also disintegrated.

"Anita's badly hurt. Unconscious." Kat's hand shot down to unbuckle her harness. "You two all right?"

"Alive," Robertson replied. "George's hurt."

"I'll live," DeMooney said. "Is she alive?"

Anita moaned.

"We gotta get her help." Kat glanced back. DeMooney's left hand held his right shoulder. Blood soaked his sleeve. It appeared the copter blade fragment had grazed his shoulder on its way to the dash. It could have been worse for him. For all of them.

Kat undid the latch and flipped up the door next to her. The rotors on her side still spun but were slowing. She instinctively covered her head as she trotted around to Anita's door.

The cause of Anita's condition and why they had crashed became evident. Part of a long narrow beak, formerly attached to a dactyl, was embedded like a lance through the cabin's door and still stuck into Anita's side.

There was nothing she could do while that beak remained lodged in the door. Kat grabbed it. Yanked hard. The beak slid out, and Anita gasped. Anita's eyes fluttered open, but her face pinched up. She was obviously in a lot of pain. Blood soaked the side of her jacket. "Not my best landing," she mumbled.

Kat smiled. Somehow, Anita maintained a sense of humor. But Kat had to do something about the bleeding. "Robertson, check in the back for an emergency aid kit."

She ripped one of her sleeves off her shirt. Pressed it against Anita's side.

After a few seconds, Robertson's head popped back up. "I don't see a kit."

"Look again!" Kat yelled.

"Oh, here it is. Under the seat." He held it out.

"Guess video stars don't need common sense. Bring it around and get out what I need. Gauze and tape!"

He opened the kit and came around, handing over a strip.

"What's this?" she asked.

"Skin patch. Haven't you heard of these, sugar?" he mocked. The "sugar" was added sarcastically. Kat found it less grating than when he had meant it as an endearment.

Skin patches were new. She had heard of them but had never seen, much less used, one.

"Well... open it!" she yelled. "In case you can't tell, I'm a little busy here."

Robertson ripped open the packaging and held out the patch. Kat pulled away her bloodied sleeve and lifted Anita's blouse.

"Oh, that's a lot of blood." Robertson's face scrunched as if the pain were his own.

Kat grabbed the patch from his hand and quickly laid it over the wound. It instantly stuck down, and the bleeding stopped. It would deliver antibiotics and a local anesthetic to help with the pain as well. It wouldn't help if Anita had internal bleeding though.

"Get another one of those out and help your boss," Kat shouted.

"Not my boss. My director," Robertson muttered as he trotted back around with a patch to help DeMooney.

Meanwhile, Kat helped Anita remove her helmet. Anita

and DeMooney still needed medical attention, but even more importantly, they all needed to get to safety. Kat had grown up around dinosaurs and could get back on her own if needed. She knew how to blend into the environment and avoid being noticed. The others, however, would stick out like ripe berries ready to be picked.

She punched the controls on the radio. Dead. The fragment stuck in the dash had taken out a lot of the electronics.

"Radio's out," she announced. "Hand me my pack. It's got a two-way radio. Won't have the range of the copter's radio, but I should at least try."

"I've got this." Robertson smiled and whipped out his cell phone.

"That won't work out here, genius."

Robertson frowned at his cell before shoving her pack at her.

"Can you reach Ridgeback with that?" DeMooney asked.

Kat pulled out the radio. "Probably not. Maybe someone else is out and about though." She tried, but there was no reply. She saw their heads sink.

Kat waded out a short distance through the thigh-high grass and sat. Had to think. She had three others to keep alive. Even Robertson.

With the broken radio, no one would even know they were in trouble until they failed to return in the evening. Rescuers wouldn't come looking until the morning, and they wouldn't know where to look. A few people might have spotted the copter heading east from Ridgeback. But it was a mighty big area. It might take most of a day, maybe even two, to find them without a signal. She would have to make it easier for them.

"Oh my!" Robertson pointed at her. "George, get the heck over here and take a look."

DeMooney stepped away from the copter, the pain reliever in the patch already clearly working its wonders. "Oh!" He pointed his video camera at Kat.

"What now?" Kat squinted.

"Ah... what you're sitting on," DeMooney said.

"It's a penta skull. So?"

"It's a freakin' dinosaur head," Robertson exclaimed.

Kat didn't understand the big deal. There were a lot of dinosaur skulls around. When the big dinosaurs died or were killed, predators or scavengers picked off the meat and ate the smaller bones, but they left the truly big bones and the skulls of pentas and rexes to litter the land.

She got up, ignoring the men as they examined the skull. Kat's concern was for Anita, so she stepped toward her.

"How are you feeling?"

"Side hurts, but I'll live." Anita rubbed her head. "My head's throbbing too. Must've banged it when I got stabbed. I think I blacked out right after."

"Lucky you had on your helmet." Kat leaned over and noticed the bruise on Anita's cheek.

"Yeah, guess so."

"Mm. Sounds like you might have a concussion." Kat stared out across toward the brontos for a moment. "Hate to ask, but you think you'll be up for a hike?"

"Hike?"

"We can't stay here. Rescue's at least a day away, and this place is... too dangerous. We need to get moving."

Anita frowned. "Where?"

"That hill over there."

"I... Yeah, I can make it."

Kat wasn't so sure, but they needed to move. "Everyone," she shouted, "grab your packs! Let's get hiking."

"Shouldn't we stay put?" DeMooney asked. "If rescue's coming, they'll be looking for the copter."

"Yeah," Kat admitted. "But the rexes are a lot more likely to find us first." Especially the one on the other side of the hill.

Robertson put his hands on his hips. "Wait. You're not taking orders from her, *are you?*"

"I hired her because she grew up here. Came highly recommended. This is her turf. Knows these animals better than any of us. So, yeah. If you want to stay alive, you should too." DeMooney pointed back at the copter. "Now grab your pack and stop acting like an idiot."

Kat was careful not to stare, but she watched out of the corner of her eye as Robertson shook his head and stomped off.

Over her shoulder, she threw her own pack loaded with everything needed for survival. Not her first night in the wilderness. She attached her holster to her thigh and her survival knife to her calf. Then she marched through the tall grass.

Not long after, she heard someone stumble behind her. Anita, down on a knee. Robertson hurried to her side and wrapped her arm over his shoulder. *Good. The son of a gun's finally helping someone beside himself.*

The pace was hard on Anita, but Kat knew they needed to reach the safety of the trees. She scanned for trouble and listened. Only the grunts from the brontos, directly in line to the hill, were heard.

Brontos were typically not aggressive toward people, unless someone got too close to one of their young. Nevertheless, she veered to the right of the herd, and they marched on.

A rex suddenly appeared at the edge of the hill to their right. It had to be the one they'd seen from the copter, and it appeared agitated. It pivoted and lumbered toward them.

Kat considered the trees ahead. Still too far—especially with Anita in her condition. The weight of the pistol rested against her thigh, but it would be useless against a monster of this size. The bullets wouldn't be capable of penetrating deep enough for serious damage. It would only anger it further as if they hadn't done a good enough job of it already.

Kat scanned around. Searched for some type of cover. Flat

grassy prairie surrounded them. Her eye turned toward the brontos. "This way!" she yelled.

Anita and the men seemed frozen.

"Run!" Kat screamed.

The rex was now in full stride. Kat raced toward the nearest bronto. It craned its small head at the end of its enormously long neck toward them. Or more likely, toward the charging rex behind them.

The bronto's tail whipped away from them. Their extraordinarily long tails were like waves of a tsunami though. They moved away from you first. Then came crashing back, and it was like getting hit by a fast-moving truck.

"Get down!" she screamed and fell flat to the ground. "And stay"—*Whoosh!* The bronto's enormous tail streaked over their heads— "down."

Kat twisted as she yelled. Watched as the others dropped too. Robertson barely in time.

She peeked over the grass. The rex stopped short. Just beyond the range of the tail. The tip streaked past the rex's snout. A sound like a gunshot rang out as the tail snapped at its end and started its return.

"We're trapped," DeMooney cried.

"This way. Follow me. But stay on your hands and knees and keep your heads down," Kat ordered.

Whoosh! The tail sailed over them again.

"Keep going," she yelled as she crawled toward the next bronto. The tail kept sailing overhead. When she stayed low, she couldn't see the rex through the tall grass. It probably couldn't see them either.

She took a quick peek and cursed. The rex circled toward the hill side of the brontos. She stopped crawling, and the others caught up.

"Seems to know where we're going. What the heck do we do now?" DeMooney asked.

"Stay put," Kat said. Everyone needed a rest anyway. Anita

breathed heavily as she lay on her back, a hand pressed against her side.

After a minute, Kat peeked over the tall grass again. The rex had gotten too close to the trailing bronto which now swung its tail too. The rex halted, out of striking distance of the bullwhip of a tail. After a few minutes, the rex backtracked away from the hill.

"Follow me." She waved forward and then again crawled toward the last of the brontos between them and the trees. Took an occasional peek at the rex. It didn't seem to know where they were though amid the brontos. She hoped it might even give up on them. After all, how long could the rex's little brain stay mad?

They were under the tail of the last bronto. The giant held its tail up and rigid, ready to whip it back and forth again if the rex returned. All the brontos remained on edge.

Kat continued toward the hill. The rex was now on the opposite side of the herd. She saw it through the brontos' legs; it seemed to have found something. A dactyl. One that had hit the copter. That meal would keep the beast occupied for the moment.

Kat stood and told the others, "It's time to run." She let DeMooney and Robertson race ahead while she threw Anita's arm over her shoulder and dragged her as they hurried together. The men almost reached the tree line, but when Kat glanced back again, the rex was still far on the other side of the brontos. Time to stop worrying about the dangers behind and start worrying about what might be ahead.

"Hold up, guys," she called out. The men stopped and turned toward her. She slowed to a walk. Let Anita continue on her own.

Kat reached down to her holster and pulled out her pistol. "We don't know what might be in these woods." She worried about raptors or juvenile rexes. Kat stepped past them and into the shade at the edge. Leaves rustled. A twig snapped. She swung her pistol to the right.

A greenback raced across the dead leaves. A theropod with a basic shape not unlike that of a rex or raptor but being the size of a turkey of Earth Prime, it posed no danger.

Kat lowered her pistol. Waved the others to follow as she climbed up the wooded bank. As she neared the summit, again leaves rustled ahead of them.

"What was that?" Robertson yelped.

"Squirrels." Kat stopped and stared up into the tall trees, making a decision.

"Squirrels?" DeMooney said. "They didn't evolve here, did they?"

"No. They were in the original Brown's Station Zone when that area got crossed over from Earth Prime. Some animals, like the squirrels, thrived and spread here. Others, like black bears, have all disappeared." Kat scanned around and removed her pack. "We'll set up camp here."

"What about that rex?" Robertson asked.

"It's gone," Kat replied. "Besides, the slopes are too steep for a big rex."

"Why are we stopping then?" DeMooney asked. "Lunch?"

"No lunch. Save whatever food you brought for your dinner." She pointed up into the tree limbs above them. "We need to build a platform up there, and we're short on time."

"Oh, you got to be kidding me," Robertson scowled.

"Nobody's going to be looking for us until morning," Kat said. "You want to sleep on the ground?"

Robertson stiffened as his eyes glanced around through the trees. Then he looked up. "How the heck are we supposed to get up there? I'm no monkey."

No. A baboon. Kat bit her lip to keep from verbalizing that. "Leave it to me." She kneeled and opened her pack. Pulled out a rope and unfolded a small saw which she handed to Robertson. "Cut down a few trees or branches we can use for a platform. They should be at least seven to eight feet long. Relatively straight. And they must be strong enough to stand on. We're going to need ten to fifteen of them. And take this." She handed over a small survival hatchet to DeMooney, which had been attached by a loop to the outside of her pack.

"What's this for? Fighting off raptors?" DeMooney stared at the hatchet.

Kat chuckled. "You wouldn't stand a chance. I'll be watching out for the raptors and rexes. That's for trimming side branches. Be as quiet as you can though. When you finish a log, drag it back here."

As the men searched for the right-size trees, Kat checked on Anita who sat with her back up against a thick trunk. "How are you doing?"

"Better. What can I do to help?"

"Just sit there. You still need rest. I'm going on a quick scouting mission along the top to make sure we're safe for now."

Anita stared after the men. "Jerk," she muttered.

"What?" Kat stopped. Did she hear it right? Was it directed at her?

"Nothing."

Kat squatted in front of her. "Something's bothering you. Talk to me."

Anita turned and stared in the direction of the men. "Robertson. He's such a pig. That jerk was supposed to be helping me back there, but he constantly had his hand on my bottom."

"You should have said something."

"I felt weak. Dizzy. And I was trying to be quiet because I thought we were in danger."

"We were." Kat crouched. Her hand went to Anita's shoulder. "But if he touches you again, you holler. Or better, punch him in the face. Okay?"

Anita gave a quick smile and nodded.

Kat stomped off to scout the area. Putting a bullet in the guy's butt would cost her, but it wouldn't be the first time she had gotten into trouble. Kat had yet to spend any time in jail though.

Over the next couple of hours, they built the platform. Kat shimmied up the tree almost as fast as the squirrels. She liked it among the branches. Safer, and she could watch out for dangerous animals from up there.

She spotted two boughs almost perfect for the base of their platform. A smaller branch jutted off a different bough eight feet above those and ran at an angle across the lower pair. She attached a pulley to the smaller branch and had the men pull the logs up and hold them while she set them in place. Spare rope served as cordage to tie them down. Platform finished, she made a fire pit by covering a small area with green leaves, dirt, and small rocks. Then firewood was hoisted up.

Then came the people. They used the rope to hoist them up. Robertson first. He was heaviest, so Kat needed DeMooney's help. Then DeMooney. Finally, Kat pulled up Anita.

From the top, Anita yelled, "Don't touch me!" Kat couldn't tell what Robertson had done. Since Anita didn't punch him, Kat figured Anita simply didn't want him near. DeMooney helped her instead.

Kat shimmied up the tree. On top, she glared at Robertson for a moment before pulling a tarp from her pack. Tied it over the branch above their heads to protect them from rain during the night. The underside was silver and would reflect heat back down to them as well. The sun was setting as they pulled food out of their bags.

DeMooney pointed his camera at the sunset. He had been sporadically shooting video footage during the construction of the platform. The guy never gave up. "This is beautiful. I wish I had a camera over that way to film us staring at the sunset." He pointed behind them.

"Can I see your camera?" Kat asked.

"Why?"

"Just hand it over."

DeMooney stretched out his hand. "All right but be careful with it. She's my baby and pretty expensive."

Kat got up and, after slipping the strap over her neck, climbed onto another branch.

"Hey! Careful with that." DeMooney stretched a hand in her direction.

Kat ignored him and shimmied along the branch, a short distance from the others. She stared a moment and then lifted the camera. They all stared at her.

"Well, don't look at me like dummies. Look at the sunset. DeMooney, point at something," she directed. "Anita, turn your head back around and smile. Perfect!" She lowered the camera and, after shimmying back along the branch to the platform, handed the camera back. Then she sat to finish her meal, legs dangling over the edge of the platform.

"This will be really good once edited for sound," DeMooney said after reviewing the footage. "I'm impressed. Who taught you to shoot like this?"

"Stanford."

"You went to Stanford? I didn't know you've been to Prime," DeMooney said.

"Yeah. I took some classes there where I learned how to use video equipment. I was eighteen when we castaways were found. A number of us were offered scholarships that year. Every school wanted us for the publicity. I had my choice of fifteen schools."

DeMooney cocked his head and stared at her. "You're full of surprises. I suppose you're going to get us a bonfire started by rubbing a couple of sticks together."

Kat laughed as she opened a small plastic container she had pulled from her bag and held up a match. "We're building just a small one. Help stay warm through the night."

That night, they curled around the flames. Kat's head butted against Anita's head. Her feet by Robertson's feet. DeMooney had his head by Robertson's head. Anita and Robertson were soon out. DeMooney complained he couldn't sleep. "What if I end up rolling off the platform?"

Robertson slept on his back and snored. Kat watched for a while by the fire's flickering. She thought about how easy it would be to give him a kick. Send him falling—especially since DeMooney's back was to the fire and her. No one would know Robertson hadn't just rolled over in his sleep.

Kat turned the other way and closed her eyes. She slept for a time before waking to add more wood to get a fire again from the dying embers.

* * *

She woke again; the sun now peeked over the horizon. Cold ashes filled the fire pit, and Kat shivered in the brisk morning air. DeMooney was already up filming the sunrise. Sitting up, she stretched out her arms. Working out the kinks in her back from the hard logs.

Robertson lay on his back, mouth open, sounding like a grunting bronto. She was sure if he'd slept on the ground, he would be in the belly of some dinosaur by now.

"It's tempting to stick something in there, don't you think?" DeMooney set his camera down. "There wouldn't be a big creepy insect crawling around, would there?"

Kat laughed, surprised by DeMooney's mischievous side. "Good morning. Sleep any?"

He shook his head. "Maybe tonight if I'm in a bed."

"I'm sure they're already out looking for us."

DeMooney nodded.

"Here." She handed him the radio. "Keep trying on channel nine. Going to get a big fire started below." She scrambled off the platform and down to the ground. Dry sticks were plentiful, and Kat piled what she'd gathered to a spot cleared free of leaves and twigs. After the fire was blazing, she smothered it with green grass still covered with dew. A large column of white smoke drifted toward the cottony clouds above the treetops. She tended the fire, adding more wood and grass. The smoke would probably be seen long before anyone heard their radio call.

Robertson finally stood on the edge of the platform, facing the other direction, urinating. She knew she was a fairly good shot and fantasized about separating a dear part of him from the rest. Anita suddenly sat up and faced the opposite direction from the men. Kat turned back to tending the fire.

DeMooney held the radio to his ear. Suddenly, he yelled, "They're coming. They saw the smoke."

It was sooner than she had thought. They must have gotten lucky where they started searching. Kat smothered the fire with dirt and then turned toward the task of getting everyone down off the platform. Fifteen minutes passed. Robertson was the last one still up top.

The thumping of the chopper echoed through the trees. By its sound, it seemed to be landing in the field by the downed quadcopter. As they lowered Robertson, DeMooney explained he'd asked to meet them there. He wanted to retrieve his other cameras. "They're expensive."

"About time," Robertson said once down. "I'm ready to leave this forsaken world to the freaking dinosaurs." He grabbed his pack and left the group staring at his backside.

"Wait," Kat called. Robertson ignored her. Stomped down through the woods. Kat waited for Anita to pack the last of her stuff.

Robertson traipsed twenty yards downhill from them when Kat glanced in his direction. Something else moved through the woods. A raptor darted toward him.

She reached for her pistol. Hesitated.

If she held her shot, no one would know she'd seen the

creature. No one would blame her. Perhaps it would be justice to let the raptor have him.

But I'd know.

Robertson's head turned toward the raptor. He screamed.

The raptor raced in his direction.

He turned to run. Kat couldn't help herself. Even for such a pathetic man.

She lifted her pistol. Fired three quick shots just before the raptor leaped. The creature's head contorted as it flew, and Kat knew one of her shots had found its mark.

The raptor was probably already dead by the time its trajectory carried it into Robertson's backside. Flattened him.

He screamed again as Kat galloped toward him. She kept eyeballing around. Another raptor appeared to her right. She stopped and fired two more shots. Bullets ripped through the chest of the second raptor. It dropped and tumbled downhill.

Kat continued toward Robertson who screamed like a hadro in the jaws of a rex. She spied a third raptor, but it darted away.

"Help!" Robertson cried. "Get it off!"

"Calm down, you big baby. It's dead already." Kat stomped toward him. Then she saw the source of his pain.

The two sickle claws of the raptor had landed and buried into him. One on each buttock. Like getting two four-inch knife blades jabbed into his backside. Kat smiled. The raptor had done it for her. She wouldn't have to put two holes back there after all.

"You know," she said as she pulled on a talon, "they say justice is blind. But, then again, sometimes it gets you right it in the—"

"Ahh!" he screamed.

"It got you good." Kat grinned. "There's quite a bit of bleeding, but you'll live." She yelled up at DeMooney. "Grab the emergency aid kit. Need patches down here."

DeMooney scrambled down with a patch a minute later.

Handed it over as Robertson rose to his feet. His hands covered where the claws had been buried.

Kat snickered. "You'll have to drop your pants for this."

Robertson cocked his head to the side. "You've got to be kidding!" He sighed before unsnapping his trousers. They fell around his ankles.

"Strange. I took you for a boxers kind of guy," Kat giggled. "The briefs have to come down too."

"Come on. Quick about this. It hurts." He lowered his underwear and bent over. "And stop laughing."

"There's only one patch left. Do you want it on the left cheek or the right?"

"What? Oh, for cripes sake, put it on whatever side looks—"

Kat slapped it on hard, and Robertson screamed. Then she yanked on her remaining sleeve until it ripped free. "Here." She held out the cloth. "Ball this up. Hold it against the other cheek."

"It's all right, Denard," DeMooney said. "You'll be fine."

Denard scowled at him. "All right! How's it going to be all right? How am I even going to be able to sit?"

"Let me have the radio back," Kat said. DeMooney handed it over. "Bert." There was only one chopper out of Ridgeback. Bert was the pilot. "Change of plans. We've injured people here. Meet us as close as you can by the hill."

"Roger that. Are the injuries life threatening?" Bert asked.

"They'll live," she replied, looking at Robertson. "We may need a soft pillow for one of them." She glanced at DeMooney.

"It's all right," he said. "I can buy new cameras. I have all the vids here on my tablet anyway. They're what's really important."

The flight back to Ridgeback was uneventful, except for Robertson's constant moaning. No pillow.

* * *

Kat refilled her glass from a bottle of chardonnay she shared with Anita. They lay on lawn chairs on a quadcopter pad. A couple of greenbacks grazed on the opposite bank of the channel. Anita commented on how she looked forward to when her new quadcopter rested where their butts now sat. They began a discussion over a new business adventure. According to Anita, whole dinosaur skulls would fetch a hefty price back on Prime. She had connections but needed Kat's skills in collecting the bones.

"Hello there," a familiar voice shouted from behind them.

They turned. "Mr. DeMooney!" Anita exclaimed.

"Ladies." He tipped the fedora from his head as he walked on the dock. "Please, call me George."

Anita gestured toward an empty chair. "What brings you back to our world? Business or pleasure?"

"Business. Always business. Miss Mendez, I have a document for you," DeMooney said as he sat.

"What's this about?" Anita asked.

"Your quadcopter. I'm here representing the network in this regard. The copter they promised is aboard the multiverse ship docked here right now. All you have to do is sign this, and it's yours. I'll have the guys aboard unload it."

"And all I have to do is scribble my signature?" Anita squinted.

"Yes. Well, there are two conditions in the fine print of this agreement you should be aware of. First, you will fly us for free around this world for one episode. And second, you will not sue the show or the network for past offenses against you by Robertson."

Anita cocked her head.

"What can I say?" DeMooney apologized. "It was written by one of the network's lawyers. Denard wasn't a perfect gentle—"

"He's a pig!" Anita shouted.

"Yeah." DeMooney sighed. "I looked the other way for way too long."

Anita stared at him. "It's here now?"

"Uh… yeah."

"I need that dang copter. Ugh!" She bit on her lip. "Oh, well! Where do I sign?"

"Right here." DeMooney unrolled and handed her his tablet. She signed with her finger.

"A copy is being sent to you automatically. Now for my primary reason for being here. Kat."

"Me?" Wine sprayed from her mouth.

"I'm here to offer you a position."

"A position?"

"We were just talking about Denard."

"What about him?" She stared hard at DeMooney.

"We had to let him go." A smile crept onto her face. DeMooney continued, "With all the lawsuits piling up, the network insisted on severing ties with him. Which brings me to you. I'm here to offer you his old job?"

"Is this some kind of prank for a reality show?" Kat searched the shore for a hidden cameraman.

"I'm totally serious." He handed her the tablet. "Here's a contract. It's all ready. Just needs your signature."

Kat's gaze turned to DeMooney. "But why me? I'm nobody in show business."

"Oh, but you are. The episode we filmed here has been our most popular one ever. We've been flooded with requests to have you back. I know when a star's been born. What do you say?"

Kat looked at the agreement.

"Have a lawyer or an agent look it over first if you like. I just want to know if you're interested," DeMooney said.

Kat knew she ought to get somebody to look at it, but then she stared at the numbers. It was more money than she thought she would make in a lifetime. "I won't need a lawyer. I accept, Mr. DeMooney."

"Please, call me George," he insisted.

"George," she replied.

"I'll be back on Monday then. Miss Mendez, please make next week available. He smiled as he stood and tipped his hat. "Good evening, ladies." Then he marched toward the shore.

Kat looked at Anita. Anita stared back, a silent "OMG" coming out of her mouth. They raised their drinks together until the glasses clinked.

"Here's to your new copter." Kat chuckled. "And let's hope this time you can keep it up in the air."

Anita frowned mock indignation. "Don't worry. As long as I don't have to carry video stars with heads so big as to weigh us down, the copter will be just fine."

Kat burst out laughing and clinked Anita's glass again as the red sun slowly sank from view.

THANK YOU

We hope you enjoyed this collection. The Science Fiction Novelists invite your feedback. If you are interested, please join us on our Facebook group page.

www.facebook.com/groups/science.fiction.novelists